Haunted.

"If you're talking about the old house on the creek," the woman behind the counter said, "folks around here have been saying it's haunted."

"Haunted." Lauren nodded knowingly. She and Kate had just joined us.

"I think these people watch too much TV," Kate murmured.

I agreed with her. Okay, I was used to Lauren's runaway imagination. But adults talking about ghosts? Give me a break!

Look for these and other books
in the Sleepover Friends Series:

Super Beach Mystery

Susan Saunders

AN
APPLE
PAPERBACK

SCHOLASTIC INC.
New York Toronto London Auckland Sydney

ISBN 0-590-43923-5

12 11 10 9 8 7 6 5 4 3 2 1   1 2 3 4 5 6/9

Printed in the U.S.A.   28

First Scholastic printing, July 1991

Chapter 1

Not too long ago, it was a Friday night, and my three best friends — Lauren Hunter, Kate Beekman, and Patti Jenkins — and I were planning on having our regular Friday night sleepover.

But before the evening was over, we knew that it was going to be anything but *regular*! I mean, how often do we get invited to spend our spring vacation in Florida, investigating a mystery?

I'd better start at the beginning. I'm Stephanie Green. Not long ago, Patti's uncle — Nick Pollard — married Tara Chipley. Ms. Chipley was our substitute teacher for a while at Riverhurst Elementary, where Patti, Kate, Lauren, and I are in fifth grade. Uncle Nick and Tara live in an apartment in the city now.

But that night, they were in Riverhurst, and had taken the four of us out to dinner at the Pizza Palace, one of our favorite places. I thought that was a big enough treat by itself, but it was only the beginning!

"How would you girls like to investigate a ghost?" Uncle Nick asked.

"What?" Lauren gasped. She's really susceptible to believing in ghosts and stuff like that. Kate says Lauren lets her imagination run away with her. Sometimes I think Kate's right. But Uncle Nick sounded serious.

"Now, Nick," Tara said. She started to explain. "Last year I inherited a little house in Puerto Delfin, Florida, from my great-aunt Mary. I haven't really decided what to do with it. Nick and I thought spending a few days down there would help us make up our minds."

"Where does the ghost come in?" Kate demanded. She always likes to get right down to the facts.

"Actually, girls," Uncle Nick said, his eyes twinkling, "there isn't *really* a ghost. But we got a phone call from a real estate agent down there, and he said that he's heard some disturbing things about Aunt Mary's house. He tried to convince us that the townspeople thought the place was haunted — and that we should sell it to *him*, cheap!"

"Of course we don't believe the place is really haunted," Tara said. "But still, we should go down there and see what's going on."

2

"We know that you girls have a week's vacation coming up," Uncle Nick went on, "and the cottage is within walking distance of a beautiful beach."

" . . . So how would you like to trade some of this cold, damp Riverhurst weather for Florida sunshine?" Tara finished with a smile.

"Would we!" all four of us shrieked. The idea of going to Florida in the middle of the school year was really exciting. I tried to put ghosts out of my mind. Instead, I thought about how I would convince my parents to let me go. After all, I wouldn't be missing any school.

"Do you think we'll see any dolphins?" Patti asked. She's crazy about dolphins; she's been studying them in Quarks, which is a science club at school.

"Sure." Tara smiled. "When I was a little girl, I spent the summers with Aunt Mary, and I remember seeing dolphins swimming in the Gulf of Mexico. They're so beautiful and graceful."

"Excellent!" Kate exclaimed. "I can take our video camera and film our vacation! It'll be great to use some scenery besides Riverhurst." Kate belongs to the Riverhurst Elementary Video Club, and is always itching to practice her filming technique.

"I can see myself now," I said. "Just lolling around on the beach, working on my tan! And I won't have to baby-sit Emma and Jeremy for once." Emma

3

and Jeremy are my twin baby brother and sister. I really love them, but they can get a little wearing sometimes. I was looking forward to just reading on the beach without worrying about whether one of them was crawling off toward the water!

I was also looking forward to spending time with Uncle Nick and Tara. They're great — not like grown-ups at all. They're still sort of newlyweds, and they're fun to be around, really nice and easygoing. Uncle Nick has blondish-brown hair that's kind of wavy in front, a thick mustache that's darker blond, and nice, twinkly blue-gray eyes behind wire-rimmed glasses.

Tara is small and slender, with reddish-brown hair that she usually wears in a French braid, cool green eyes under perfectly curved eyebrows, and a perky sort of nose with light freckles across it. I was sure that they wouldn't worry about when we went to bed, or whether we were eating too much junk food. Going to Florida with them would be almost like going by ourselves, just the four of us!

Lauren finally broke in. "Can we go snorkeling in the ocean?"

"Absolutely!" Tara said. "In fact, there's a coral reef just offshore."

Lauren was practically strapping her flippers on already! Patti and Kate looked excited about it, too. That's when I started thinking about electric eels, stingrays — and weren't there major alligators in Florida, too?

"And for a different kind of entertainment, Wonderworld Theme Park is only a couple of hours away," Uncle Nick said. That did it! A trip to Florida was too good to pass up for *any* reason — not even ghosts and weird sea monsters!

"Wonderworld! All riiight!" The four of us shouted in unison. Wonderworld is super-neat. It has the world's tallest roller coaster, the longest water slide, and a bunch of other great rides.

"It's all set, then," Tara said. "Nick and I will talk to your parents and make sure you can go. Then all we'll have to do is pack. I know the six of us are going to have a fabulous vacation together!"

I couldn't wait to call my parents and ask them. After dinner, Uncle Nick and Tara dropped us off at Lauren's house because it was her turn for our regular Friday night sleepover.

Lauren asked her parents if she could go, then the rest of us took turns calling our parents for permission. They all said yes! We told them that Uncle Nick and Tara would be calling with the details.

"Florida, here we come!" I shouted. For the rest of our sleepover, we talked about what we would take with us, how great it would be to lie in the sun, how great it would be snorkeling in the Gulf. We couldn't think of anything better than the Sleepover

Friends taking a vacation together.

One for all and all for one — that's us. Besides being in the same class, 5B, at Riverhurst Elementary, we take turns having a sleepover at one of our houses almost every single Friday night. In fact, it's hard to remember when we weren't spending practically every waking moment together.

Until this past fall, though, Patti didn't even live in Riverhurst. And I've been here less than two years myself.

I moved to Riverhurst from the city at the beginning of fourth grade, when my dad got a job here. I met Lauren when we were both in the same class last year.

Lauren and I hit it off right away. Then she introduced me to her friend Kate Beekman. Lauren and Kate have been best friends since they were babies, although they're exact opposites in a lot of ways. Lauren is tall, with dark hair, and Kate is short, with blonde hair. While Lauren is really easygoing and sort of a slob, Kate likes everything in order, and is perfectly neat. Somehow Kate and I rubbed each other the wrong way at first.

But Lauren wouldn't give up on her plan to make Kate and me close friends, too. She fixed things so that the three of us ended up riding our bikes to and from school together. Soon I was surprised to find myself inviting Kate along with Lauren to a Friday sleepover at my house.

I guess things went well enough for Kate to ask me to *her* house the following Friday night. One sleepover led to another, and before long we were the Sleepover Trio.

Even then, things weren't perfect. Three is kind of an awkward number — somebody is always feeling left out. So I was really pleased when Patti showed up in Mrs. Mead's room this year. I knew Patti from the city, where we were in the same first-grade class. She's even taller than Lauren, with wavy brown hair. She's quiet, but lots of fun, and you couldn't meet anyone nicer.

Kate and Lauren liked Patti from the start — who wouldn't? So when I wanted her to be part of our gang, they both said "yes" right away. Fifth grade had barely gotten off the ground, and suddenly there were four Sleepover Friends!

To get ready for our trip to Florida, Lauren and Patti signed us all up for snorkeling lessons at the Riverhurst Health Club. While they were excited about learning to snorkel, I was a little nervous about what we might meet once we moved from the small club pool into the great big ocean.

I mean, Lauren's the sort of person who'd probably want to get into a race with a swordfish. Or hitch a ride on a manta ray. I don't think she's afraid of anything physical. And Patti is so interested in learning about ocean wildlife that she wouldn't think twice about getting personal with a six-foot jellyfish. But I'm definitely more comfortable with just reading about those things in books!

Anyway, it was our last lesson, and Kate and I were pretty tired. While Lauren and Patti kept swimming, we pulled ourselves out of the pool to sit on the edge. "Have you decided what you're taking yet?" she asked me. When I shook my head, she teased, "It's only a week until we leave for Puerto Delfin. You'll need at least that long to pack your suitcase."

I grinned and shrugged. "Uncle Nick said to keep it to just one suitcase, because of space, so I'll just have to take the bare essentials," I said.

"Uh-huh. Like fourteen pairs of shorts, and fifty-nine different tops . . . agh!" Kate yelled as I kicked my fins and covered her with a major wave! I can't help it if I'm the most fashion-conscious of my friends.

Chapter
2

The following week, I tried to put ghosts and sharks out of my mind and focus on clothes. We would be driving from cold, wet northern weather into hot, damp southern weather, so I had to bring both winter and summer clothes.

It was hard knowing what to take. I finally decided to take four pairs of shorts, six different tops, and two bathing suits. I hoped there would be a washing machine at Tara's house. I also packed one T-shirt dress, one sundress, and one dressy skirt and top set, in case we went out to eat at a fancy place. Then I shoved six pairs of scrunchy socks and plenty of underwear into all the loose places in my suitcase. I decided to wear my sneakers on the trip and pack my rubber flip-flops and dressier sandals. Almost all my clothes are red, white, or black. Those are my favorite colors.

Nana and Dan were in town visiting us for a few days. Nana is my grandmother, and Dan Kessler is her new husband. They offered to take me shopping to make sure I had everything I needed. Even though I was already mostly packed, I couldn't resist. First we stopped at Just Juniors at the mall, and I found a really great pair of red bicycle shorts — on sale, too. I decided that I could squish them into my suitcase somehow. Then we went to the drugstore and got some sunscreen and a cute travel-size shampoo and conditioner. Last, they bought me a book of stamps so I wouldn't have any excuse not to send a postcard to them.

Our last day of school I could hardly sit still — I was dying to get started on our trip! In less than twenty-four hours we would be on the road to Florida! It was impossible to pay attention in Mrs. Mead's class. Before we left school for the day, I got some of my friends' addresses, like Jane Sykes's and Hope Lenski's, so I could send them postcards.

Finally school was over, and the four of us set off on our bikes together. The sleepover was at Patti's that Friday, natch. Uncle Nick and Tara were staying at the Jenkinses', too, so that we'd all be together and ready to leave early the next morning.

Lauren had to go ahead to Brio Drive, and Kate and I turned off on Pine Street. "I'll see you in a few hours, Patti!" I called as I waved good-bye. Patti lives over on Mill Road.

I was so happy when I dumped my schoolbooks on my bed and knew that I wouldn't have to look at them for a week. I double-checked my suitcase to make sure I hadn't forgotten anything. My dad was lending me his camera, and Mom had given me two rolls of film.

After dinner my parents drove me over to Patti's, and I jumped out of the car almost before we had stopped. They both got out and hugged and kissed me good-bye.

"Catch a big fish for me, sweetie," my dad said.

"I will, Dad," I promised.

"Try to call us on your way down," my mom added. "And be sure to let us know as soon as you get there. Don't forget, Stephanie."

"I won't," I said. "And you call me, too." Tara had given all our parents the address and telephone in Puerto Delfin. They also knew which motel we were planning to stay in on the way down.

I reached into the backseat and kissed Emma and Jeremy good-bye. "Take care of yourselves, guys," I said.

"Don't be a nuisance to Tara and Nick," my mother added as Dad started the car. "Be sure to do your own laundry, and clean up after yourselves, and . . ."

11

"We will, Mom. See you in ten days!" I called as they backed down the driveway.

When Patti opened the front door, she rushed me inside. "Come on in before you freeze," she said. "Lauren and Kate are already here." Lauren was early for once!

Patti's house has two stories and a huge attic, where we can make noise without bothering anybody. Usually we grab an armload of sleepover snacks and head straight upstairs. But that night we hung around in the living room with Uncle Nick and Tara, Patti's mom and dad, and her little brother, Horace, so we could talk about the trip.

Tara had brought an old photograph album with her, with pictures of herself and her family when she was little. She showed us what Puerto Delfin used to look like.

"The town is pretty small," Tara said. "It hasn't really grown much in the last twenty years. It's on the edge of the Gulf of Mexico." She held up a photo taken from above.

"It's pretty!" Patti said. Palm trees and flowers grew everywhere around small houses that were painted in lots of different colors, like pink and green and blue, and the water sparkled beyond them in the distance. I was glad I'd remembered to take my sketchpad and watercolor markers.

"Which house is your aunt's?" Kate asked Tara.

"Oh, you can't see it in this picture," she said, flipping a few pages. "It's on the outskirts of town, next to a creek. . . . Here it is." Tara pointed to a photograph of a square house perched on round stilts, with pale yellow shutters and a screened-in porch. It sat in the middle of a perfect bright green lawn, surrounded by a white picket fence draped with purple blooms.

"Wow!" Horace said. "Look behind it — it's like a real jungle!" He pointed to a jumble of odd plants, bushes, and trees on the far side of the fence. It looked like the setting for a Tarzan movie.

"Yes, Aunt Mary didn't clear away all the brush on the rest of her property — which is about ten acres — because she didn't want to disturb the birds and animals that lived there," Tara said.

"It'll be great to explore!" Lauren said happily.

"Are there snakes?" Horace asked hopefully. "Maybe you can bring me one back, Patti." Horace is an okay kid for a six-year-old, but he has this disgusting collection of "pets" in the Jenkinses' basement: turtles, salamanders, frogs — those kinds of things. Yuck!

"When I stayed with Aunt Mary," Tara said, "she had a tame king snake living under the house for a while."

"Ew!" I shrieked. What were we getting into?

"Don't worry, Stephanie," Tara said. "I have a

13

high school student, Carl Withers, who's keeping the grass cut short around the house. That should discourage snakes. Actually, Nick, we ought to call Carl and let him know we'll be there on Sunday."

"Good idea — he can check to make sure the electricity has been turned on," Uncle Nick said.

Tara turned the page of the photo album. "I'm thinking about presenting the property to the town as a wildlife preserve," she said, "in Aunt Mary's memory. Here she is, in her favorite hat."

"That's Aunt Mary?" Lauren said, sounding surprised, although I didn't see anything that unusual about a white-haired lady in a straw hat with a floppy brim.

"Um-hmm, standing next to the creek, where the dolphins used to swim," Tara answered.

"Dolphins? Really?" Patti said. "Do you know what kind?"

Tara shook her head and smiled at Patti. "The last time I saw them I was only twelve, and they all looked the same to me. But they still may be hanging around. Dolphins can live for quite a long time, can't they?"

"As long as fifty years," Patti said.

Just then Kate poked me with her elbow and nodded at Lauren, who was bent over the album, trying to get a better look at Aunt Mary. "Do you have any other pictures of her?" Lauren asked.

"On the back of this page, I think," Tara replied, flipping it over. Lauren was still peering at the old lady's face intently. She finally looked up and caught Kate's eye. Kate lifted her eyebrows in a silent question.

"Later!" Lauren mouthed, looking very mysterious.

"Why don't we go upstairs and catch a few minutes of dedications?" I suggested. On Friday nights, the Riverhurst rock radio station takes requests over the phone, which can be kind of fun. But I was also curious about what Lauren had on her mind, *or* her imagination.

"Dedications. Good idea," Kate said, picking up on my idea right away. "Come on, you guys," she said to Patti and Lauren.

"Thanks for showing us the album, Tara," I said. Patti leaned over and kissed Uncle Nick and Tara good-night.

"See you in the morning, honey. Bright and early," her uncle warned. "Six o'clock." We all groaned loudly, and Mr. and Mrs. Jenkins laughed.

On our way upstairs we stopped in the kitchen to get some sleepover snacks. Lauren "Health Food" Hunter grabbed an apple and a banana. The rest of us normal people got a bag of pretzels, a bag of gingersnaps, and a jar of peanuts.

"What was that all about, Lauren?" Kate asked

15

as we dug through the cabinets for glasses and plates. "Why were you staring at Aunt Mary as though she had two heads or something?"

"Didn't you watch *Stranger Than Truth* last night?" Lauren replied breathlessly. "Aunt Mary looks *exactly* like the ghost in that Florida story, 'The Ghost and Mr. Simpkins'!"

Kate and I burst out laughing. "Come on, Lauren!" Kate said.

"I'm serious!" Lauren said, plopping a handful of paper napkins down on one of Patti's trays. She turned to face us, her eyebrows creased in a thoughtful frown. "This man named Mr. Simpkins lives somewhere in south Florida. And for the last year, his house has been haunted by — "

"Let me guess — a little old lady wearing a straw hat?" Kate collapsed in giggles on a kitchen chair. As I said, it doesn't take much to set off Lauren's runaway imagination.

"Okay, no straw hat," Lauren admitted with a grin. "But maybe it's not so funny! After all, Tara inherited the house a *year* ago, didn't she?" Lauren nodded wisely. "For all we know, Mr. Simpkins lives in Puerto Delfin, right down the road from Tara! The drawing they showed of the ghost on TV looked *exactly* like Aunt Mary. Didn't you guys think so?"

"I think I dozed off as soon as I heard the theme

music," Kate said, just to tease her. I hadn't seen it, either.

But Patti had. She thinks it's important for a scientist to keep an open mind. "Now that you mention it, that photo of Aunt Mary did look something like the drawing, Lauren," she said, filling glasses with ice for us. I couldn't tell if she really thought so, or if she was just trying to make Lauren feel better. "Cherry Coke, or Dr Pepper?" Patti asked.

"Cherry Coke. Anyway, Lauren, it seems to me it's good news if Aunt Mary's ghost *is* haunting Mr. Simpkins's house," Kate said with a straight face.

"Good news?" Lauren squawked.

"Sure. That way, we won't have to worry about running into her where *we're* staying," Kate said, and she and I both started giggling again.

"Lauren, do you want something to drink?" Patti interrupted before Lauren could get huffy.

But even Patti was grinning, and finally Lauren was, too. "Okay, okay. Dr Pepper, please," she said. "But I'm keeping my eyes peeled."

"All we'd have to do is put on our snorkel gear, and we'd scare any ghost completely out of the state," I said as we started up the stairs.

Up in Patti's attic, we listened to WBRM for a while, but nothing much was happening with the dedications. So we trooped downstairs for refills on our drinks. We were just about to push open the kitchen door when Patti stopped us, finger to her lips. We could hear Tara talking on the phone, and she sounded upset.

"What do you mean, Mrs. Withers?" she was saying.

"That must be the mother of the boy who mows the lawn," Patti whispered.

"Surely Carl doesn't believe those ghost stories!" Tara said.

"What did I tell you?" Lauren hissed, her eyes wide and round.

"Yes . . . yes . . ." Tara said. "But . . . when was the last time Carl was actually at the house?"

The four of us outside the door weren't moving a muscle, because we didn't want to miss a word.

"Six weeks ago? The lawn hasn't been cut in six weeks? Did he at least check to see if the electricity had been turned on? What?! Even *you* didn't want to go into the house?" Tara was beginning to sound really irritated. "Fine. We'll put a check for the twenty-five dollars we owe you in the mail. I can't wait to get to the bottom of this nonsense. Goodbye." She hung the phone up angrily. "Ghost stories!" she said to Uncle Nick, who was standing next to her. "What next?"

"I hope there hasn't been any trouble at the

house," Uncle Nick said. "Maybe it's not such a good idea, driving the girls down there without knowing what we're getting into."

"Oh, no!" Patti whispered. I gulped. We weren't going to miss out on our Florida vacation, were we?

But Tara said to Uncle Nick, "I'm sure everything is fine. I'm not willing to disappoint them. Carl Withers probably just decided he'd rather work on his tan than mow the lawn, so he came up with a ridiculous excuse."

"Okay, hon," Uncle Nick said. "You're right. Let's not even mention it to the girls, then."

"Right!" Tara said.

"They're coming," Patti whispered, and the four of us dashed upstairs again on tiptoe.

"Don't start, Lauren!" Kate warned firmly as soon as we were back in the attic and could safely discuss it. "You heard what Tara said — it's nothing more than a lazy high school boy."

"I'm sure Tara and Uncle Nick are right," said Patti. "And we don't want to not go to Florida just because the lawn didn't get mowed, do we?"

It was a little creepy, but I guessed not. Anyway, Kate and I both said, "No way!"

Lauren cocked one eyebrow, then finally smiled. "No way," she said.

* * *

19

We went to bed pretty early, but before I knew it, Patti's mom was shaking us awake. "It's a little before six," she said. "Hurry and get dressed. There are blueberry muffins and fruit salad in the kitchen."

"It's so dark out there," I moaned as Kate and I rolled out of our sleeping bags. "Could I have just ten more minutes?"

"You can catch up on your beauty sleep in the car," Kate said, instantly wide awake. She's definitely a morning person. She's also never late. And her hair's never out of place, even after a night of sleeping on the floor. It's kind of depressing.

"You definitely don't want to get left behind this morning, Stephanie," Patti said. She and Lauren were sharing the double bed, and Patti was staring out the window. "Oh, my gosh, it's snowing!"

"Snowing? This late in the year?" I said. "Florida, here I come!" I scrambled to my feet so fast that Kate, Patti, and Lauren burst out laughing.

"You're moving faster than you did in the school relays," Lauren giggled as I sprinted toward the bathroom with my toothbrush.

The weather cleared a little while we were eating breakfast. But I was glad I'd brought along my fat down jacket when we started loading Uncle Nick and Tara's green minivan.

"Everything here? All five suitcases?" Tara said, peering into the back of the van and counting under her breath. Uncle Nick and Tara were sharing one.

"Check," said Uncle Nick. "And six sleeping bags strapped to the roof."

"And six people," said Mr. Jenkins. "Get in, girls." He gave Patti a big hug, and the rest of us, too. "Have a wonderful time, all of you."

"Will we talk to you this evening?" Mrs. Jenkins asked Uncle Nick.

"As soon as we get to the motel," he promised. "Now, we'd better hit the road if we want to reach the Florida state line before dark." Our motel was just on the other side of it.

Horace was all bundled up in one of Mr. Jenkins's jackets, with his racing-car pajamas peeking out at the bottom. "I want to go, too," he started to sob, and Patti sort of choked up herself. "You can go next time, Horace," she told him. "And I'll bring you a snake back, I promise." *Oh, great,* I thought.

"Wait!" Lauren yelped. "Do we have the snorkeling equipment?"

"Tucked in under the seats," Tara said. "I packed it myself last night."

More good news — I'd really have hated to leave behind our beautiful snorkeling masks, and miss out on the fashion statement of the season. I squeezed into the third seat next to Lauren and two suitcases. Kate and Patti climbed into the second seat — and we were ready to roll.

21

Chapter 3

You learn a lot about people when you travel with them. Like Uncle Nick's secret thirst for adventure. We'd barely gotten out of Riverhurst when he turned off the interstate to travel on the backroads. "I go for the more exciting routes," he explained.

Right away we got stuck behind an oil truck creeping along on a slick, curvy, two-lane highway, so it took us about an hour to go thirty miles.

"At this rate we'll get to Florida just in time to turn around and come back," I murmured to Lauren. But she was sound asleep, propped up against her suitcase — Lauren can sleep anywhere. Since it wasn't even eight o'clock in the morning yet, I closed my own eyes and dozed off, too.

I woke up when the van stopped. I raised my head and saw that we were parked outside a diner.

"I'm running in for a second cup of coffee,"

Uncle Nick announced in a low voice, because Lauren and Patti were still sleeping. "What about you and Stephanie, Kate?" We shook our heads, and I went back to sleep.

We pulled back onto the road and started to make good time. By noon we'd driven through three whole states and pretty far into a fourth.

Traveling really makes you hungry! We were all starving when Uncle Nick stopped in front of a cute restaurant called the "Galley-Ho."

"This should help us get in the mood for Florida," Uncle Nick said as we piled out of the van.

I'd almost forgotten about Kate's vacation video. But now she dragged the camera out of her tote and started directing us.

"Wait, Stephanie — don't move yet. Let me get focused," Kate said, scrambling out and pointing the camera at me. "Okay — climb out slowly. . . ."

Just then I caught my sneaker on the buckle of Patti's seat belt, and almost did a double-flip onto the pavement! Luckily, Patti grabbed me by the shirt on my way down. "Are you okay?"

"Wipeout!" Lauren said, and we all burst into giggles.

"Start it over," I said to Kate.

"But what a great beginning for the video," she argued. "It's got humor, and action, and — "

"Start it over or find a new star," I said firmly.

"Don't look at me!" Lauren said to Kate.

"Me, either," said Patti.

Kate sighed and rewound the cassette. "Take it from the top, Stephanie," she said. This time I didn't stumble over my own feet.

We crossed a little gangplank to get to the front door of the Galley-Ho. Inside, the restaurant was decorated with underwater scenes, like a plastic treasure chest, fishnets, glass floats, starfish . . . and a giant rubber squid about ten feet long!

"Look at the size of that thing!" Kate said as we followed the waiter to our table. "Maybe we'll run into one of those on the reef."

"Are giant squids really that big?" Lauren asked once we'd sat down right underneath the rubber one.

"Bigger — they can grow to almost fifty feet," Patti replied.

"F-fifty feet?!" I squeaked, while Kate was exclaiming, "Excellent!" She was no doubt thinking of her video star — me — having a wrestling match with one of them! Ten arms against two!

But Patti went on. "They only live in the deepest parts of the ocean. And all of those stories about them grabbing ships and swallowing sailors whole are probably made up, since the biggest thing they eat is fish the size of herrings or mackerels." Probably? They didn't know for sure?

We looked at our menus and ordered our

lunches. Then Tara pushed back her chair and said, "Nick, I'm going to call the electric company in Puerto Delfin — to double-check on our lights."

While Tara was gone, we glanced around the restaurant. It seemed to be a pretty popular place — almost every table was full. But some people stood out. . . .

Lauren spotted him first. "Wow!" she exclaimed under her breath. "Doesn't he look just like Matt Pacelli?" Matt Pacelli is the lead singer for the B29s, and a real hunk!

Patti, Kate, and I turned around to see who she was talking about. She was right! Younger, though. This guy looked about sixteen.

I shook my head. "Too conceited," I said. How could somebody who looked that good be anything else? "I think the younger one's cute, though." The Matt Pacelli look-alike was sitting at a table with his parents and a boy about our age.

"Who?" Lauren said. She, Kate, and Patti hadn't even noticed the younger boy. Probably no one did when his older brother was around. He had brown hair, grayish eyes, and a cute, lopsided grin.

Tara came back from the phone sounding more cheerful. "The electricity was switched on at the house on Wednesday," she told Uncle Nick. "No problems at all."

I looked over at the boy's table again after we'd

all been served. The parents and the two boys were studying a road map. I wondered where they were going. Too bad we'd probably never see them again — the United States is a big place.

They left long before we'd eaten our lunch. We piled back into the minivan and hit the road again. The weather was still pretty dismal. But that afternoon Uncle Nick's route followed the coastline of the Atlantic for a couple of hours. And seeing an ocean, even a cold one, always improves my mood. As long as I'm not *in* it.

I took the sketchpad and watercolor markers out of my tote, and did some sketching as we drove along: sea gulls, fishing shacks, grass-covered dunes — whatever popped into my sight. Or brain.

Before I knew it, I had sketched the face of the cute boy in the restaurant.

"Ooh, Stephanie," Lauren poked me. "Is Willie Judd already a thing of the past?"

"Aren't you glad you came?" Kate added. "We're not even halfway to Puerto Delfin yet, and you've already thrown over the Juddster."

"Don't be dumb," I said. "Anyway, we'll never see those people again." I scribbled over the boy's face and started to sketch a fishing boat. Little did I know what was in store for us. . . .

Finally, at about sunset, we pulled into the motel. It was called The Colonial, and it was enormous.

There were two restaurants and a snack bar, an indoor pool and an outdoor pool, and even a miniature golf course. Neat!

But we'd been on the road for twelve hours. Even though we'd just been sitting in the car all that time, we were too worn out to do anything more than drag ourselves and our stuff into our two-room suite . . . and collapse.

Uncle Nick ordered room service — burgers for everybody. As soon as we'd eaten, we took turns calling our parents. Then Patti, Lauren, Kate, and I crawled into the two king-size beds in the bedroom, and Tara and Uncle Nick pulled out the foldout couch in the living room. We all slept like bears until seven o'clock the next morning.

Right after a big breakfast, Uncle Nick said, "Ready to hit the trail, gang? Next stop, paradise!"

The four of us detoured through the lobby just long enough to buy some postcards to send to our parents. We were standing next to the registration desk, writing, when we couldn't help overhearing someone in a nearby phone booth saying, "Dolphins? No — don't you have something more unusual? Everyone has dolphins nowadays. . . . Yes, I want something different. . . ."

Lauren and I looked at each other and raised our eyebrows. "Oh, yes," Lauren said in a fake snobby voice. "I have two dolphins myself. They came with our pool." Kate, Patti, and I all snickered. Then Kate frowned, and said, "Hey, you guys. Isn't that the same woman we saw at the Galley-Ho? The cute boy's mom?"

We all turned to look at the woman in the phone booth. Sure enough, it was! And there was the cute boy, walking toward her. He really did have a nice smile.

I kind of wanted to stay and maybe say hello, but Kate grabbed my arm and started pulling me up the stairs — we had to hurry back to our rooms and pack. Upstairs, I folded my nightshirt, threw my toothbrush into a plastic Baggie, and closed my suitcase. Then I set it down neatly by the bedroom door. I picked up my down jacket and headed out again.

"Where are you going?" Kate asked me.

"Oh, I wanted to buy one more postcard, to send to Nana and Dan," I said.

"Yeah, right," Lauren said, smirking.

"I'll meet you guys outside the revolving doors in the lobby," I said. "Make sure my suitcase and sleeping bag get into the van, okay?" I rushed out before they had a chance to tease me anymore.

When I got back to the registration desk, though, the phone booth was empty, and the cute boy was nowhere around.

Oh, well, I thought. As my grandmother would say, "Nothing ventured, nothing gained." Just then my whole gang trooped across the lobby and out the revolving doors, so I wandered across and joined the line. But as I was pushing through, I saw the boy with the cute smile, pushing on the other side! As we whirled past each other, I had the feeling he remembered me from the restaurant.

But I didn't have a second to dwell on it. I shot out of the revolving doors. Uncle Nick and our group were already waiting at the curb by the green minivan, and there was Kate with her video camera stuck out the window, recording the whole thing.

The kid was nice about it — he actually waved at the camera before he disappeared in the direction of the snack bar. But I could have strangled her.

"Kate, honestly. You don't have to record every facet of my life, do you?" I growled as I crawled over the suitcases and into the backseat next to Lauren. I'm sure my face was as red as my sneakers.

"Did you talk to him?" Lauren asked.

"Did he talk to you?" Patti wanted to know.

Tara said, "He certainly has a nice smile."

"We just happened to pass each other in the revolving doors," I replied, frowning at Kate. "No big deal." As far as I was concerned, that was that. Boy, was I wrong.

Chapter
4

All morning long, we drove through Florida. We saw Jacksonville, Gainesville, and Ocala. Ocala's surrounded by farms with beautiful horses. There was a pirate ship in the harbor at Tampa, the *José Gasparilla* — it was neat.

We were heading farther south, and the weather was definitely warming up. When we got to Fort Myers, it was time to take off my down jacket and roll up my sleeves. We had lunch at a little sidewalk cafe, where we ate club sandwiches and watched people shopping in the boutiques along the waterfront.

"Last leg of the trip," Uncle Nick said when we loaded into the van again. Sure enough, about an hour and a half later we finally rolled into Puerto Delfin.

"Riverhurst seems a million miles away!" Patti said. We were driving down a road lined with palm trees, past the pink and blue houses we'd seen in Tara's photographs.

Then we went around a curve, and the blue-green Gulf of Mexico spread out in front of us. Little waves splashed up on a white, sandy beach, and kids were casting their fishing lines from an old wooden pier.

"I can't wait to get into that water!" Lauren said.

"Neither can I!" Kate, Patti, and I said at exactly the same time.

"I think we'd better get settled at the cottage before you guys hit the beach," Uncle Nick said with a grin. "Don't you, honey?"

Tara was staring out the window with a pleased smile. "When I came down here last year, I was so upset about losing Aunt Mary that I didn't take the time to really look at anything in town. It's hardly changed at all!" she said. "There's the Majestic Movie Theater, where I went to the movies with my brother Gil on Saturday afternoons, and Haines's Grocery. Nick, we'd better stop and buy some supplies before we drive on to the house."

We pulled into the parking lot beside the grocery store and helped Tara make a shopping list. "I'm sure we'll have to come back for things, but at least this will get us through the evening," she said. She started writing in a little spiral notebook, "Hot dogs, buns, mustard, relish, milk, juice . . ."

"What about a broom and a mop?" Uncle Nick suggested.

"Definitely," Tara agreed. "Mop, bucket, cleansers, and so on." By the time she'd finished the list, it was three pages long.

Tara and Uncle Nick took one page, gave a page to Patti and me, and handed the last page to Lauren and Kate. "We'll meet at the register," Uncle Nick said as we walked into the store and grabbed shopping carts. "If you see anything not on the list that appeals to you . . . go for it." He's great.

Patti and I got the page that had mostly food on it, and we added a few items that were definitely appealing to us: fudge-ripple ice cream and a bag of pretzels.

As we pushed our loaded cart up to the register, we heard Tara asking the woman behind the counter, "By the way, do the Haineses still own this store?"

"Oh, no — they retired about five or six years ago," the woman said. "It belongs to Mr. Grandy now. He owns Grandy's Grand." When Tara shook her head, the woman explained, "Used to be the old Buccaneer Hotel?"

"Oh, I know the Buccaneer," said Tara.

"Say, you haven't been in Puerto Delfin in a while, have you?" the woman said.

"Not really, not in almost fifteen years," Tara admitted with a smile. "I came here often when I was a child, to visit my great-aunt, Mary Matheson."

"Mary Matheson," the woman repeated. "No, it doesn't ring a bell."

But it rang a bell with one of the other shoppers, an older woman with curly gray hair. "Miss Matheson passed away last year, didn't she? She lived in the little house on the creek," the older woman said.

"That's right," Tara said. "Did you know her well?"

The gray-haired woman shook her head. "Only by sight."

"I'm thinking of offering the property to the town of Puerto Delfin as a wildlife preserve, in memory of my aunt Mary," Tara said. "We've driven down here to come to a final decision about it," she added.

The gray-haired woman lowered her voice. "Well, you couldn't *pay* me to go near the place. Especially not after dark. And if I were you, I'd drive straight back to where I came from!" She pushed her cart quickly away from us.

Tara frowned and watched the woman walking away.

"Some people will believe anything," Nick said, pushing his cart up next to us.

"If you're talking about the old house on the creek," the woman behind the counter said, "folks around here have been saying it's haunted."

"Haunted." Lauren nodded knowingly. She and Kate had just joined us.

33

"I think these people watch too much TV," Kate murmured.

I agreed with her. Okay, I was used to Lauren's runaway imagination. But adults talking about ghosts? Give me a break!

"Why on earth would anybody say that?" Uncle Nick asked the woman at the counter.

"I don't know, personally," she replied. "I live on the other side of town. But it seems people have seen strange lights near the creek. And heard some weird sounds. Maybe you'd better talk to the mayor, or the sheriff, before you try to do anything with the property," she advised.

"Haunted!" Lauren repeated to Kate, Patti, and me. "What did I tell you about Aunt Mary?"

As the woman started ringing up our groceries, a short, plump man with a blond crew cut hurried over to us. "Did I hear you say that you're the owner of the Matheson property?" he asked. "I'm Greg Grandy. I own Grandy's Grand Hotel, as well as this fine grocery store, and I'm a real estate agent here in Puerto Delfin." He took Tara's hand and shook it. "And you are?"

"Tara Chipley," she said. "This is my husband, Nicholas Pollard."

"Ah, yes. I believe I spoke with you by phone several weeks ago. Ms. Chipley, Mr. Pollard." Greg Grandy beamed at them, and right away I thought there was something phony about him. Wasn't he being a little too friendly?

"Now, it's only fair to tell you that you're going to have plenty of problems unloading the Matheson place, as Lois here might have explained," Mr. Grandy rattled on. "But I just might be willing to take it off your hands if the price is right — "

"I have no plans to sell it, Mr. Grandy," Tara cut him short.

"So I heard you say. But I think you'd have a lot of trouble deeding it to the town." Mr. Grandy smiled smugly. "It has quite a spooky reputation — ghosts and so forth."

Tara drew herself up. "I don't believe in ghosts, Mr. Grandy," she said stiffly. "And if there are any problems, we intend to clear them up."

"I'm sure you do, Ms. Chipley. But let me give you my phone number." Greg Grandy dug around in the pocket of his pale blue jacket and pulled out a business card. "You might want to call me once you've sorted things out."

Tara dropped the card into her shoulder bag without even glancing at it. But after he'd strolled away, Tara looked at Uncle Nick and shook her head.

"Curiouser and curiouser," Uncle Nick said.

"It certainly is," Tara said, looking at us. "I'll never forgive myself if I've involved you girls in any kind of sticky situation."

"All this ghost stuff is ridiculous," Kate said.

"Yeah," Patti said. "It takes more than that to keep the Sleepover Friends away!" She looked at me and Lauren. "Right, guys?"

Lauren and I looked at each other. Deep down, I think all this ghost stuff was starting to get to both of us. But we couldn't let down our friends. I nudged Lauren in the ribs.

"Right!" I said enthusiastically. I could handle ghosts, I told myself bravely.

"Yep!" Lauren said, forcing a smile.

Tara hugged all four of us at once. "You girls are great. Let's get to the bottom of this!"

But when we were loading the bags into the minivan, I found I was in for something *much* worse than a dumb old ghost.

"We can fit some of the groceries in here," Uncle Nick was saying, unlocking the back flap and pushing it up. "We seem to have more room back here than I remember."

"Hey, wait a minute!" I said. "How many suitcases do we have?" I *knew* for a fact that we *didn't* have any leftover space! I quickly counted. "One, two, three, four — four! Where's the other one? Where's mine? Oh, no!" I wailed. "My suitcase is missing!"

Chapter 5

"Your suitcase? How could it be missing?" Uncle Nick said, flabbergasted. "The van was locked while we were in the store."

"I don't know! Wait a minute — did you guys load it into the van at the motel?" I asked Patti, Lauren, and Kate.

"We carried everything in our room out to the sidewalk," Lauren said. "I'm sure of it."

Patti nodded. "I double-checked."

"Well, it's definitely not here." Tara had climbed into the van to look. "When did you last see it, Stephanie?"

I tried to remember exactly. "On the bed at The Colonial this morning. I stuck my nightshirt inside it — and my toothbrush and toothpaste and shower cap. Then I closed it, zipped it up, and . . . set it down near the door to the living room."

"Near the door?" Uncle Nick said.

"I guess it was sort of behind the door," I admitted, "because there wasn't much space between the door and the end of my bed. Then I grabbed my jacket and went out to — "

"Buy another postcard in the lobby," Kate said.

"Right." But I'd run into the boy with the nice smile, and I'd gotten so flustered, I hadn't even thought to check in the van for my suitcase before we drove away.

"It's all our fault," Patti said forlornly. "You asked us to make sure your sleeping bag and suitcase got into the van."

"There *are* six sleeping bags here," Uncle Nick said, counting them on the roof of the van.

"Yeah, I left my sleeping bag with the others in the living room," I said glumly. I'd packed and repacked that suitcase twenty times, to be sure I'd have just the right clothes! Now I was stuck with the jeans I had on, a shirt that was already too hot, red sneakers, and a down jacket — not exactly what I needed for Florida!

"Oh, dear," Tara said, smoothing my hair down. "This trip isn't really getting off to a good start. I hope things pick up from now on." She thought for a few minutes. "There's a phone booth inside the store. Why don't I call The Colonial right now and ask them to put Stephanie's suitcase on the next bus to Puerto Delfin?"

"Righto," Uncle Nick said.

"In the meantime, you can borrow clothes from the rest of us," Kate said. "Although I didn't bring anything in red or black."

"I didn't, either, but I know we'll be able to find something for you to wear," Lauren said generously. But Lauren is inches taller than I am!

"Yeah — think of it as a fashion adventure," Patti joked. Patti's the tallest girl in our class. Her sleeves would hang down to my knees!

"That's the spirit, girls," Uncle Nick smiled.

"Great . . . thanks . . . you guys," I said, trying to sound as cheerful as I could. Anyway, I'd probably get my suitcase by the next day at the latest. . . .

But after Tara had reported back from the phone booth, I wasn't so sure. "One of the cleaning people found your suitcase right after we left this morning — the manager was holding it in the office," she said. "But there's no direct bus connection between there and Puerto Delfin. I'm really sorry, Stephanie, but the suitcase will have to switch buses in Jacksonville, and again in Ocala. And there's only one bus a day going south from Sandringham" — that's the town where The Colonial Motel is — "and we've already missed it for today."

39

"So you'll have your clothes by day after tomorrow," Kate said briskly. At least Kate is my size, more or less.

"It'll be a fun change," I said doubtfully, hoping I sounded enthusiastic. We all piled back into the van.

"Which way from here?" Uncle Nick asked Tara, maneuvering the van out of the parking lot.

"To the right, down Front Street, then left on Ocean Drive," Tara directed. She swiveled around to talk to us in the back. "I hope you girls aren't nervous about what those women said in the store. Sometimes when a house stands empty for a while, people get funny ideas about it."

"There was a house like that behind Lauren and me, in Riverhurst," Kate said.

"Even my new house on Brio Drive looked spooky before we moved into it and fixed it up," Lauren volunteered. Which is true — before the Hunters got their hands on it, it looked a lot like Nightmare Mansion on "Friday Night Chillers."

"That's right. As soon as someone starts living in it again, things go back to normal," Tara explained.

I knew *I* wasn't going to feel normal until I had my own suitcase and all my clothes back!

"Oh, dear — they've torn down the old ice-cream parlor," Tara said, staring out her window.

"But the courthouse looks just the same. There's the sheriff's office. And the old Buccaneer Hotel." The Buccaneer was a four-story stucco building painted blue and white. Now a large sign across the top announced in pink neon, GRANDY'S GRAND HOTEL.

As we turned left, Lauren suddenly poked me sharply with her elbow. "Check out the furniture store on the corner!"

"Simpkins's Buried Treasures?" I read the name painted on the plate-glass window. "So?"

"Simpkins is the name of the man who was being haunted by the old lady in the straw hat!" Lauren whispered. "On *Stranger Than Truth*!"

"Lau-ren!" She was starting to weird me out a little.

"Did you know a Mr. Simpkins, Tara?" Lauren asked casually.

"No, I don't think so," Tara replied. "That store was owned by the two elderly Simpkins sisters."

"See?" I said to Lauren. Maybe it was losing my suitcase, or not meeting that cute boy, or all the ghost stories, but the more things that went wrong, the more determined I was to be cheerful. I wasn't going to let this stuff get me down! We were in Florida, we were all together, nothing was going to stop me from having a good time!

"We're almost there!" Tara said. "It's just through that wooden gate, and up the drive."

The van rolled up the gravel driveway and stopped beside the front gate. Then we all just sat there for a few seconds, taking it in.

Kate had her video camera ready to shoot, but she was too surprised to push the button. "Wow," she said, at a loss for words — for once.

"It's — so green," Patti said softly.

It was green, all right. There was so much green stuff growing around the house that it was almost hidden by it! Waist-high grass, weeds with stalks the size of your wrist, baby palm trees, oaks, and pines, and the whole mess covered with tangles of bright green vines!

"Something tells me that it's been a lot longer than six weeks since Carl Withers has been here!" Tara said.

"It's certainly very . . . tropical," Uncle Nick said.

I may not believe in ghosts, but I sure remembered Tara telling us about the king snake under the steps. The whole place looked like Snake City.

"Do we . . . uh . . . get out?" I asked. *Or do we roll up our car windows and drive straight back to Grandy's Grand Hotel?*

But Tara was hopping out of the van to run up the mossy front steps of the house, and Uncle Nick was right behind her.

So the rest of us climbed out, too.

Tara pulled a set of keys out of her shoulder bag and started to stick one into the old-fashioned lock on the front door. Then she paused, and stood back a step.

"Something wrong, honey?" Uncle Nick asked.

"Well, I'm not sure, but . . ." Tara stepped forward and gave the door a shove. It swung open with a creak.

"Someone's been here before us," Lauren whispered hoarsely. She turned and looked at me, Kate, and Patti, as if to say, *What do you think about ghosts now?*

Uncle Nick pushed the door open wider. "I bet this is where our 'ghost' problem started," he said. "It looks like someone broke in."

I felt sorry for Tara. She was just standing there, unsure of what to do.

"Honey, why don't I take a quick look first, okay?" Uncle Nick asked. Tara nodded. We watched him disappear into the darkness of the house. When I glanced over at Kate, I saw her eyes were gleaming. I groaned to myself. Why do I have the kinds of friends who think mysterious houses are exciting?

Uncle Nick soon popped back out the front door. "It seems okay," he said. "But, Tara, it looks like some furniture may be missing."

Tara took a deep breath and stepped inside. The four of us Sleepover Friends crowded in behind her, and Uncle Nick brought up the rear. I figured there were bound to be fewer creepy-crawlies inside the house than outside.

We found ourselves in a large, square room that must have been the living room. There was an old couch with flowered cushions and a matching arm-chair. A wrought-iron coffee table stood in front of them. There were also some bookshelves with dusty books, and a rocking chair. Some paintings of beach scenes hung crookedly on the walls. Everything was covered with dust, and the air smelled musty and damp.

Tara walked over to a window and threw it open, then stood and looked around the room. "I think you're right, Nick. Aunt Mary had a round oak table in the far corner, and it's gone. And there used to be some glass figurines on top of that bookcase." She turned to look at us. "I think we have the answer to our ghost. People breaking in and stealing stuff would account for the noises and the mysterious lights at night. They probably wouldn't be hauling stuff away in the daytime." For a second, Tara looked as if she might cry.

"Can you tell if anything else is missing?" Uncle Nick asked gently, flicking the overhead light on. Thank goodness we had electricity. Tara started to look around more closely.

Kate leaned over and whispered in my ear, "Maybe I should change the title of my vacation video from *Florida Fling* to *Florida Nightmare*. Stephanie, how would you feel about starring in a thriller about — "

"Forget it, Kate!" I said, frowning at her. Couldn't she see how upset Tara was?

"The four wooden chairs that matched the table are missing, too," Tara was saying. She walked across the living room and through a door. "The bedrooms are off this hall. Let's see how those are."

There were three small bedrooms, two right next to each other, and a third, larger one across the hall from a small bathroom. "These two bedrooms are okay," Tara told Uncle Nick. "Musty, but okay. Twin beds in each, with white iron headboards. But Aunt Mary's room had a brass bed in it — it's gone now. And a tall chest of drawers is missing, as well." She was throwing open curtains and windows as she went, and sunlight and fresh air came flooding in. It helped make the place look a little less creepy. But I could tell we had a major cleaning job ahead of us. "Let me check the kitchen," Tara said, disappearing down the hall again.

The kitchen was straight out of a corny old TV show: an ancient black-enamel stove, a rickety table with a gray metal top, a dented white refrigerator

45

with its door hanging open, some worn-out pots and pans, and — my heart sank — no dishwasher or washing machine in sight!

But Tara was relieved. "It's all here," she said. "Even the blue roasting pan that Aunt Mary filled with birdseed every morning." She closed the refrigerator door, then leaned over and plugged its cord into an outlet. Instantly the old motor started humming, which was a good sign. At least we'd be able to keep our sodas cold!

"So as far as you can tell, the things that are missing are a dining room table and chairs, a brass bed, and a tall wooden chest of drawers?" Uncle Nick asked.

"That's right," Tara said. "And the glass figurines."

"Okay. I'm calling the sheriff," Uncle Nick said. "I think he'd better come out here and take a look around."

"The phone is in the big bedroom," Tara told him. She unbolted the back door and pushed it open. The jungle that we'd seen in the photographs looked a lot closer than I'd imagined. Where was the ocean, anyway?

Uncle Nick was back in a second, shaking his head. "The phone isn't working," he said. "Let's load up and drive into town, to the sheriff's office. I can get in touch with the phone company while we're there. And call everybody's parents.''

"Could you find the sheriff's office by yourself, Nick?'' Tara said. "Girls, you go with him. I'd like to stay here and start making the house a little more livable.''

"You'll be okay?'' Uncle Nick asked.

"Of course, I will. Our burglars have taken everything worth taking — they won't be back,'' Tara said, smiling weakly. "Go ahead,'' she added to the four of us. "I know your parents are anxious to hear from you.''

"I'd like to stay here and help Tara,'' Patti said. "Uncle Nick, you'll call Mom for me, won't you?''

"Well . . . sure,'' Uncle Nick said.

"I'll give you my number too, okay?'' said Kate, pushing back her sleeves. If there's one thing Kate really enjoys, it's neatening up a messy place. She's been dying to get her hands on Lauren's room for years.

I fall somewhere between Kate and Lauren in neatness. But I couldn't breeze into town and leave Kate and Patti working. "Me, too,'' I said. "Would you just tell Mom and Dad I'm fine?''

"And mine.'' Lauren was already scribbling her telephone number on a piece of scrap paper she'd found on the counter.

"Are you sure?" Tara said to us.

"Absolutely. We'll be living here, too, Tara," Kate pointed out sensibly.

"I think I'll try to buy a couple of camp cots for us while I'm at it, Tara," Uncle Nick said, heading back down the hall toward the living room again. "The girls have the twin beds in the two front bedrooms, but you and I are without a place to sleep."

Thank goodness nobody was going to have to bunk on the floor — I'd already noticed two large, weird-looking bugs. "I'll be back in a flash!" Uncle Nick hurried out the front door.

"Before we tackle the house, I'd like to show you girls the way to the beach — take you past the creek, and point out the reef," Tara said to the four of us.

Uh . . . did that mean slogging through the jungle outside?

Lauren and Patti both yelled, "Great!" Patti added, "Maybe we'll see some of Aunt Mary's dolphins."

"Or run across some clues of your burglars," Kate said, grabbing her video camera.

I certainly wasn't going to stay in that house by myself. I lined up with the others as Tara smeared us with some kind of stinky bug repellent. Then I followed them out the door, preparing myself for a whole new world of unpleasant surprises.

48

Chapter 6

"Aunt Mary always kept a machete on the back porch," Tara said, opening the back door.

"What's a machete?" Lauren asked.

"Kind of a cross between a knife and an ax. Here it is." She picked up this enormous sword-type thing that looked more like it belonged to a dangerous pirate than a little old lady!

"Yipes!" Kate said.

"Is that to protect us from snakes?" I added nervously.

Tara burst out laughing. "Snakes are a lot more afraid of us than we are of them. The minute we set foot outside, they'll all head for cover. No, this is to help clear the dirt path that winds through the jungle to the beach. Ready?"

"Ready!" Lauren and Patti chimed together. Kate and I nodded a little less enthusiastically.

We followed Tara and the machete through the porch and down the back steps. "Pull your socks up as high as they'll go, and roll your sleeves down," she instructed. "Just about the most troublesome animals we'll run into around here are — "

"Crocodiles?" I asked, looking at the jungle ahead of us.

"No," Tara said with a laugh. "Mosquitoes."

She wasn't kidding! The minute I stepped off the porch into the weeds, I was surrounded by swarms of buzzing bugs. But the stinky bug repellent must have worked, because none actually landed.

"Don't let me forget to buy more Bugaway," Tara said, giving a bush in front of her an experimental *thwaack!* with the machete.

"I wonder if they sell Bugaway by the gallon," Kate said. For all of her teasing, Kate isn't that much more outdoorsy than I am.

"I know there's a path here somewhere," Tara said, staring down at the ground to either side of her. "But everything has grown so much. . . ."

"Is that it?" Patti pointed a little to the left, where we could just make out a faint trail threading its way through the jungle.

"Good eyes!" Tara said. "Let's stick close together." Like i might really consider wandering off by myself.

It was pretty rough going. The palms and pines

and vines were growing so thickly that we soon lost sight of the house, and couldn't yet see the creek.

We could hear the creek, though — croaks and splashing that Tara said were bullfrogs or snapping turtles. And we could definitely smell it. It was sort of like the smell of the water we'd drained out of the old swimming pool at Lauren's new house, which we figured had been sitting there for ten or fifteen years, slowly turning into green slime.

Patti was in heaven, though. Right away she spotted an oriole's nest overhead, and some special kind of fern on the ground. "What a field trip this would make for the Quarks!" she said.

"Or a survival-training camp!" Lauren added, balancing on a thick rotting log. "Kate, you ought to get some shots of this."

"Too dark, " Kate said, trying to push a vine out of her way. I heard her murmur something like, ". . . Can't believe we're out here without rubber hip boots. . . ."

Tara held a thorny palm frond aside so we could edge safely around it. "It's strange, but it looks as though someone has cut down some of the brush recently," she said. She pointed out a skinny little pine tree lying on its side next to the dirt path, its needles turning brown.

"The burglars?" I suggested, looking over my shoulder.

"While they carried a big table and four chairs away on their shoulders?" Kate shook her head.

"Probably Carl Withers, on his way to the beach instead of mowing the lawn," Tara guessed. "It can't be much farther to the creek." She gave a thick, loopy vine a good *thwock* with her machete. Then, "Ooops!" She suddenly stopped short. Kate, Lauren, Patti, and I were walking so closely together that we practically ran right over her. "Don't fall in!" Tara warned.

"Yuck!" said Kate.

Double-yuck! Aunt Mary's creek made Lauren's old swimming pool water look like a clear mountain spring!

The water in the creek was dark green, at least the part in the middle was where you could actually see the water. The areas closest to the banks were covered by thick, foamy scum, like yellow-green whipped cream. While we were standing there, pointy little heads popped up through the scum, and beady little eyes checked us out, then disappeared again, leaving ripples behind in the foam.

"Frogs and turtles," Tara said. "And maybe a few water snakes for Horace. Gil and I used to keep a dip net up in that old cypress tree. . . ."

Snakes? "How far are we from the beach?" I asked nervously. I didn't think snakes would be into making sand castles and getting a tan.

"The creek winds around and doubles back on itself a couple of times before it ends at the ocean," Tara said. "But the path is a lot straighter from now on. We'll be there in a few minutes."

It was shady and dim in the jungle, and the air was absolutely still. I was getting hotter and stickier by the second, but we trudged forward.

All of a sudden Tara stopped dead and motioned us to stop. We followed her gaze as she peered through the thick undergrowth.

"What is it?" Lauren whispered, taking hold of my arm.

"I don't kno — " I started to say, then froze into silence as I saw what Tara was looking at!

A tall, dark figure was striding through the undergrowth, straight at us. We all stood there like statues. I, for one, was scared out of my wits. Was it the burglar, who had come back to get something else? Was it the ghost?

"Uh-oh," I heard Kate say very softly. Tara straightened and held up the machete threateningly. I looked over at Patti and her eyes were just as round and scared as mine were.

Then Tara called out, "Stop! Who are you? What are you doing on private property?" The figure halted. I tried to make out what he looked like, but there were too many trees in the way. Suddenly, he turned and started running away from us.

He crashed through the small trees and ripped through the vines as fast as he could. Then he disappeared into the dim light of the woods. I let out a deep breath and looked around, to make sure we were still all together.

Tara lowered her machete and looked at us. She looked kind of shaken, too.

Lauren plopped down on a log and wiped her forehead. "Boy," she said. "What in the world was *that?*"

"An abominable swampman?" I squeaked.

Kate put her shoulders back and said briskly, "Nonsense. Just a passerby who wanted to take a shortcut through Tara's property. Nothing to be scared of. Nothing at all."

Tara smiled. "I don't know who it was, but he's definitely gone now," she said. "Let's get out to the beach quickly."

I couldn't have agreed more! We started trudging purposefully down the overgrown path. Then I heard Tara start giggling. "Imagine," she said. "Your fifth-grade substitute teacher just chased away an intruder with a machete. They didn't teach me that in college."

We all burst out laughing. Put like that, it *was* kind of funny. It would make a good story when we got back to Riverhurst, too. Laughing about it made me feel less scared.

Finally we stepped out of the trees, and it was like a different world. A cool sea breeze was blowing in off the Gulf, and the sun was so bright that it hurt our eyes.

The beach stretched away from us, clean and white, and covered with seashells in all different sizes and colors. We all breathed a sigh of relief to be out in the open and the sunlight.

As sea gulls screeched and dived overhead, Tara reached down to pick up a handful of shells. "When I was your age, I made necklaces out of these," she said. "See the perfect little round holes in the ends of them? Some sort of tiny creature drills into the shells to eat the little animals that live inside."

"The holes are just the right shape and size for stringing on colored yarn," I said, kneeling down to scoop up some round yellow shells and some pink and white scalloped ones. I put them carefully in my pockets. "I'll make necklaces for my mom, and Nana, and the twins. You could make one for Melissa, Kate." Melissa is Kate's little sister.

Kate made a face, but I noticed that she picked out some shells, and so did Patti.

Lauren was shading her eyes and squinting at the glittering water. "Can we see the reef from here, Tara?" she asked. I guess Lauren was still determined to have us all strapped into snorkling gear, looking like geeks, before we could say, "Twenty Thousand Leagues Under the Sea"!

That's when I thought of a plus side to leaving my suitcase behind at The Colonial. True, I might be able to borrow some of the clothes I needed from my friends. But I could make a fuss about not feeling comfortable in anybody else's extra bathing suit. And with no bathing suit, I'd have no frizzed hair, no wrinkled-prune skin, no meetings with sharks on the reef.

"It looks like high tide right now," Tara told Lauren. "At low tide, you'd be able to see the reef about thirty feet offshore, directly between us and the lighthouse in the distance. See where those waves are breaking?"

I was looking forward to the lazy day I'd be spending, sketching and sunbathing and stringing necklaces on the warm, dry beach, while everybody else was dressing up in masks and fins and snorkeling until they dropped. But Tara said, "We'll drive into town early tomorrow morning and buy you a bathing suit, Stephanie, so you won't have to share. I know you wouldn't want to miss out on our first trip to the reef." I forced myself to smile and nod. So much for plan number one. It looked like I was just going to have to quit being a chicken about snorkeling.

Tara was untying her sneakers and pulling off her socks. "Take off your shoes and roll up your jeans, girls!" she said. "Let's see what the water's like!"

"Hang on, Stephanie — I want to get this on film," Kate said, pointing the video camera at me as I scrunched through the sand toward the Gulf.

It's not easy being a star. I knew the water was going to be icy cold — it was only spring, after all. I held my breath as I edged closer to the waves, a frozen smile on my face. . . .

Then I looked so surprised that everybody started to laugh! It was hard to believe, but stepping into the Gulf was like stepping into a warm bathtub. Plus, the waves weren't trying to pound me to death, the way they do on the East Coast. They brushed softly against my legs, no harder than my cat, Cinders, does.

"Excellent!" I said, splashing my feet happily in the luscious warm water. "Really excellent!" With Kate filming me, I felt like one of those travel ads on TV.

"Fabulous!" Kate agreed, forgetting all about her video project as soon as she stepped into the water herself.

Patti and Lauren were already in the Gulf over their knees, kicking and splashing water around. "I can't wait until tomorrow!" Lauren said.

I was beginning to think I really did want to buy a bathing suit the next morning, even if I couldn't find one in red, black, and white. If I still didn't want to snorkel, I could at least swim around a little, near the shore.

The five of us splashed around for about fifteen minutes, enjoying the water, the sun, and the safe feeling of being out of those woods. Then Tara said, "The sun is starting to set. We'd better go back to the house and start getting organized. I want to tell Nick about our mystery guest in the woods. I hope he found something out from the sheriff."

We sat down on the beach, waving our feet in the air to dry them before putting our sneakers back on. It was nice having the place all to ourselves. Tara had told us that there aren't any direct roads to get to the beach — you either had to walk or take a four-wheel drive.

As I was tying my sneaker I heard a rattling noise in the distance and looked up. The others did, too, and we saw an old camper bouncing across the sand. It rolled to a chugging stop not far from us.

"I bet they're fishermen," Tara guessed. "Right here at the mouth of the creek, the fishing is really good."

A dark-haired heavyset man with a crew cut climbed out of the driver's side of the camper. He had a cigar stuck in the corner of his mouth, and was wearing a dirty white T-shirt. A thin woman with frizzy, whitish-blonde hair got out of the passenger side. They both stared hard at us for a moment. Then the woman gave a brief wave, and they walked around to the back of the camper and pulled out two fishing poles.

Tara finished tying her shoes. "Maybe I should go talk to them," she said. "If they fish here often, they may have noticed somebody suspicious hanging around who we should tell the sheriff about." We all got up and headed over there with her.

The man had already cast his fishing line into the surf and was watching it intently. But the blonde woman was looking in our direction again. "Hello," she called when we got close enough. "New to these parts? Just on vacation?"

"No, not exactly," Tara answered. "I'm Tara Chipley, and this is my niece Patti, and her friends. We're staying in a cottage at the other end of the creek. It used to belong to my great-aunt."

The woman frowned and looked surprised for a split second. Then she smiled and nodded. "Well, good for you. Most folks around here avoid the place. Claim there are ghosts — or worse. I'm Beatrice Goodwin, and that's my husband, Nathan," she added as an afterthought, pointing at the dark-haired man.

"We've heard the stories," Tara said.

"And you weren't impressed," Beatrice said

with a tight smile. "Well, Nathan and I don't take any chances. It's a pretty secluded spot. Don't know what you'll run into around here."

I gulped, thinking again of the figure in the woods.

Beatrice continued, "We won't give up the fishing around here because it's plenty good. But we always clear out before it gets dark. How long will you be staying in your aunt's house?"

"About a week," Tara told her. "You haven't seen anyone hanging around the creek, have you? Or anything out of the ordinary?"

"Like I said, people give the creek a wide berth," Mrs. Goodwin said shortly.

"Beatrice!" her husband boomed out as he reeled in his line. "You gonna spend the evening gabbing, or are you gonna bring me the bait bucket?"

"Why don't you get it yourself?" Mrs. Goodwin yelled back. "Have a good visit here in Puerto Delfin — you're braver than I am," she added as she turned to join her husband.

Patti, Lauren, Kate, and I glanced at each other. These people were pretty creepy.

Not for the first time, I wondered what exactly we had gotten ourselves into when we came on this "vacation."

Chapter
7

Tara decided to follow a bank of the creek back to Aunt Mary's house instead of taking the trail home. We all agreed. "Keep your eyes peeled for clues to tell the sheriff," Tara told us. *Don't worry*, I thought. In fact, all five of us were craning our necks so much, looking all around us, that we must have looked like a bunch of giraffes.

It turned out that we *didn't* see any clues, but we *did* see something a lot more exciting.

At the Gulf end, the creek is wider, and the water is clear. "That's because of the tides," Tara explained as we left the beach behind. "Fresh ocean water from the Gulf flows in and out pretty freely here. Then, as the creek winds around and narrows down farther inland, there's a lot less movement of the water."

"So dolphins would swim into the creek on a

high tide, chasing fish that flowed in with the water?" Patti asked.

"Right," Tara said, pulling her machete out of her belt to give a couple of whacks to a prickly bush blocking our way. "Aunt Mary started feeding the dolphins with fish she'd caught. After a while, she had actually trained the dolphins to come when she whistled."

"Neat!" said Kate.

"Of course, they might have come anyway," Tara went on. "Dolphins are very friendly — they're always interested in human beings — and curious. And they whistle themselves, to communicate with each other. Who knows what Aunt Mary's whistles might have meant in dolphin language?" she added with a smile.

The four of us giggled. "Maybe something really funny," said Lauren.

"Or totally rude," I said. "Like, 'Is that your nose or a banana?' "

"Let's try whistling up some dolphins!" Patti said. "It's still high tide, isn't it, Tara?"

Tara peered down at the water level in the canal in the dim light. "It looks high," she said.

"Then there might actually be some dolphins in here," Patti said excitedly. "Whistle, guys!"

Now I wasn't exactly thrilled with the idea of

hanging around this place — even though Tara *did* have her machete. But the others were all excited, so I got ready to pucker up. Kate got her camera ready, just in case. Then we crouched down next to the creek, puffed our cheeks out, and whistled as loudly as we could.

I felt sort of silly, but even Tara was doing it. With all five of us whistling at the same time, any dolphin within a couple of miles should have come running — swimming, I mean.

But we blew until we were all out of breath and red in the face, and nothing happened. "Too bad," Tara said, standing up at last. "I guess Aunt Mary's dolphins have moved on."

Lauren was crouched down next to me, so I heard her murmur, "I just hope Aunt Mary's ghost has gone with them." She definitely hadn't given up on the ghost idea! The sun was starting to set, the shadows were longer and darker, and there were odd rustlings and peeps and squawks all around us.

I guess Tara wanted to reassure us, because she said, "It's just the birds settling in for the night, you guys."

Then it happened. We had just stopped for the fifth or sixth time, while Tara hacked at more bushes and vines with the machete. We were lined up on the creek bank: first Tara, then Patti, then Kate, Lauren, and me. I squatted down to retie a sneaker and pull my socks up higher against the mosquitoes, when suddenly I heard a loud sigh.

As casually as I could, I shifted around a bit to squint over my shoulder into the gloom behind us. I didn't see anything that wasn't a tree or a bush or a vine. Besides, the sigh had sounded as if it were not more than two or three feet away.

Anybody that close would have to be in the creek! Could our dark intruder have snorkeled up in back of us? I felt as if I were going to jump out of my skin, but I also didn't want to alarm the others. If it turned out to be nothing, I would look pretty silly. I decided I was getting as bad as Lauren, letting my imagination run wild. *Pull yourself together, Stephanie!* I scolded myself silently.

I started retying my other shoe, and there it was again. A loud sigh. This time, I happened to be glancing down at the creek in front of me. I noticed a ripple moving slowly across its surface in my direction.

I froze in fear. What the heck was that? An alligator? A python? An alien creature from the deep?

Then I saw it . . . a head, rising out of the dark water! The round face was turned straight toward me, and mournful brown eyes looked into mine. The mouth curved up in a sorrowful half-smile. The eyes blinked at me once, twice . . . and before I could do anything more than try to swallow, he sank silently down into the water again, and was gone.

I tried to stand up slowly, but my knees were shaking. Had I really seen anything? Was my imagination playing tricks on me? I glanced over at Kate and Patti. They didn't look any different — they sure hadn't seen anything. Maybe it was just a combination of shadows, or the round top of a snapping turtle's shell, or . . .

Then I looked up at Lauren. She was standing as straight as a tree, frozen into place, with an absolutely horrified expression on her face. Her gaze was locked on the water in the creek, right where I'd been looking. She shivered, her head turned slowly, and her eyes met mine.

"EEEAAHH!" Suddenly we both screamed as loud as we could and stampeded up the creek bank!

"Look out!" Kate shrieked as Lauren almost ran her down.

"What is it?" Patti yelled as we tore past her.

Tara jumped out of our way in the nick of time, or she would have ended up in the creek with whatever that thing was!

Lauren and I couldn't stop — we had to get out of those woods *fast*. We charged straight through the prickliest bushes, got tangled in the thickest vines, and never slowed down. I could have stepped right on a python and never known the difference. I just wanted to put as much distance between myself and the creek man as fast as I could.

We burst out of the jungle, charged through Aunt Mary's back gate, and thundered up the back steps and into the kitchen, only to see a dark figure coming out of the hall by the bedrooms, heading straight at us!

"AAAIIIEEEEE!" we screamed again. We ran right past him, out the front door, down the front steps, and out to where the van was parked in front of the house. We threw ourselves panting against the van and tried to get one of the doors open.

"Whoa, whoa!" Uncle Nick came dashing out of the house after us. "What are you doing? Why did you run past me like that? Are you okay? Where are the others?"

Just then, Tara, Patti, and Kate came huffing and puffing around the side of the house. They jogged up to us as Uncle Nick reached us.

I was panting and gasping, and my throat still felt tight with fear. I looked over at Lauren, and she still looked pretty shaken, too.

"What on earth happened to you two?" Tara exclaimed worriedly.

"What was that all about?" Kate added crossly. Her face was all pink from running, and sweat was dripping down her forehead. "Did you guys see something?"

Tara put her hand on my shoulder. "Stephanie, did you see that intruder again?"

"Intruder? What intruder?" Uncle Nick said, looking alarmed.

Tara sighed and looked us all over. "Come on, you guys. Let's go inside, have a nice cold glass of lemonade, and fill each other in on what's been happening."

Five minutes later we were all sitting on the front screened porch with our lemonade. I sort of didn't want to talk about the weird face I had seen — but Lauren *had* seen it, too. I mean, *both* of us couldn't have imagined it, could we?

"Now, girls," Tara said in her schoolteacher voice. "Tell me what happened out there."

Lauren and I looked at each other. "Well," Lauren began uncertainly.

"Don't tell me you saw a ghost!" Kate said impatiently.

"It wasn't a ghost — and I saw it, too," I blurted out.

"Most of him was underwater," Lauren began. "He had sad brown eyes . . . a bald head . . . big shoulders . . . and a strange sort of smile, and — "
It was *exactly* what I had seen.

Kate interrupted her. "Lauren, there were lots

of dark shadows on the creek by then," she said. "It could have been a turtle, or a bullfrog, or a floating log. . . ."

"No. He sighed," I said, feeling like sighing myself.

"Who sighed?" Patti asked, sounding really interested.

"The man, or whatever he was, in the creek," I replied.

"Well, maybe it was a dolphin," Tara said, leaning forward to hear our story.

"I really don't think it was a dolphin, Tara," said Lauren. "Dolphins have long, pointy noses, and this thing didn't."

"Maybe it was a man in a wet suit," Uncle Nick suggested.

"No — he was all the same pale color, even his face. Almost grayish," I said slowly.

Patti asked, "Can you draw what you saw, Stephanie?"

I hadn't thought of sketching him. "I think so," I said slowly. I could still see that round, wet head.

"You have a sketchpad in your tote, right?" Patti hurried toward our bedroom. I looked around at the others kind of sheepishly. Now that we were all together, safe and sound, I was starting to think that Lauren and I had been silly, and that there was a perfectly reasonable explanation for the thing in the creek.

Patti ran back with my sketchpad and markers. "Go ahead," she urged. Out of the corner of my eye I could see Kate raising one eyebrow. But I ignored her and started drawing.

I drew his big brown eyes, his round head, and a low brow with sort of a crease in it. "Make his cheeks fatter," Lauren directed, looking over my shoulder. I drew fat cheeks, and that sad smile. . . .

"He sort of needed a shave, too," Lauren said. So I added whiskers around his mouth and chin. I drew in his neck, sloping down to big shoulders just barely poking up above the water.

Then I handed the sketch to Patti, and Tara and Uncle Nick crowded around to see. "Amazing!" Patti exclaimed. "You actually saw this?"

I thought again about how scared I had been when I saw it, and had looked up to see Lauren's face frozen in horror. "Yeah," I nodded. "That's pretty much what he looked like."

"Wow!" Patti said excitedly. "Do you know what this is? You guys actually saw a manatee!"

"A manatee?" Kate repeated, puzzled.

"You mean you know what we saw, and it's something that really exists?" I said.

"Absolutely! But there aren't supposed to be any in this part of Florida. This is amazing!"

Uncle Nick studied my drawing. "You know, I think Patti's right. Our own manatees — far out! Listen, I have a college friend, Warren Poole, who's a biologist for the National Parks Department in Washington, D.C. Tomorrow morning we'll drive back to town and call him for advice."

"Manatees are endangered, aren't they?" Tara asked.

"Yes," Patti answered. "We should definitely contact the authorities."

By that time we were all starving, so we took a break to get some dinner. Uncle Nick and Lauren pulled a wooden picnic table up onto the screened porch, and Tara opened cans of baked beans and cooked some hot dogs.

Kate and I quickly swept the porch clean and set the table. When we were all sitting together and chowing down, it was Uncle Nick's turn to tell us what happened to *him* that afternoon.

"So, did you find the sheriff, Nick?" Tara asked, helping herself to a second hot dog.

He nodded. "Yes, we must have just missed you guys — he followed me back and took a look around. He left right before Lauren and Stephanie came tearing out of the woods." Uncle Nick grinned widely at me and Lauren. "His name is Sheriff Gunn," he continued, "and he wants a complete written description of the missing items. He's going to circulate it to the antique stores in the area to find out if any of the furniture has turned up. He'd heard the rumors about ghosts, of course. He said they started about three or four months ago, and aren't unusual when a house has been empty for a while."

Exactly what Tara had said. Then Uncle Nick's face turned grim. "I found out why our phones aren't working, too. Our lines have been cut, right outside the house."

"Cut!?" Tara exclaimed, her eyes growing wide. She met Uncle Nick's gaze, then looked down at us. Ghosts, intruders, cut wires — what was next? I shivered, and looked around at Lauren, Kate, and Patti. Even Kate looked uncomfortable.

Then Uncle Nick continued. "But Sheriff Gunn assured me that his men will be keeping an eye on the place. We won't have anything more to worry about from now on."

"Except for our mysterious intruder," Tara said with a sigh. When Uncle Nick raised his eyebrows, she quickly told him about the dark figure we had seen in the woods, and how he or she had run away when Tara yelled.

Uncle Nick frowned and said, "Hmm. Well, it was probably just a kid taking a shortcut to the creek. Now that the sheriff is on the job, I'm sure we can sleep safely tonight."

Famous last words!

Chapter
8

After dinner, Uncle Nick disappeared into the closet in a corner of the kitchen to tinker with Aunt Mary's hot water heater. We had discovered when we started to wash up that it wasn't really working.

"At least the wiring in the house seems to be in pretty good shape," he said, poking his head out of the closet. "So what if we can't take hot showers? At least we have lights, right?"

Speak for yourself, Uncle Nick! I thought.

Tara said, "Please make it work, Nick."

After wrapping electrical tape around some wires, and tightening a couple of tiny screws, Uncle Nick did make the hot water heater work. "I can't guarantee there'll be a lot of hot water," he said. "We'll have to give it plenty of time to heat up again between one shower and the next. Who goes first?"

"You go first," Tara suggested with a smile. "It's only fair."

"Right — after all, you fixed it, Uncle Nick," Patti said.

The four of us helped Tara sweep out the big bedroom, then set up the camp cots and spread out the sleeping bags on them. "One thing to always remember when you're in Florida is to check for insects before you put on your shoes or climb into bed," Tara told us, unzipping the sleeping bags and giving them an extra shake.

"What kind of insects?" Lauren asked.

"L-like that one?!" Kate said in a strangled voice, pointing down at the floor.

"Iiiick!" The four of us were off the floor and balancing on a camp cot like acrobats.

"No, that's just a palmetto bug," Tara said calmly. It was only the biggest, grossest bug I've ever seen in my life! "It won't hurt you," she added, picking up the broom and kind of scooting it out of the bedroom like a hockey puck.

"Aren't there leash laws in Florida?" Kate murmured, and all of us started to giggle.

Tara swept the bug out the back door. Then she explained that scorpions were what we had to watch out for. "They like to hide in dark places in the daytime, and you don't want to get stung while you're putting on your sneakers. Now — who wants to sleep where?''

"Stephanie and I should share a bedrooom,'' Kate said, "because I'll probably be lending her the most clothes.'' As I mentioned, we're closest in size — both shorties.

Sharing a room with Kate was fine with me, but I sort of wished all *four* of us could sleep in the same room. The latest news about the phone wires being cut was really scary. But I tried to put it out of my mind — otherwise I knew I'd never get to sleep.

Kate and I spread our sleeping bags out on our beds, after shaking them so hard I thought they were going to rip. Then I checked to make sure that both screens on the windows were latched. I wondered if I could stand to have both windows shut and locked, too. I decided it would be just too stuffy and musty.

With the waits in between, it took quite a while for all of us to get showered. Lauren went after Tara, then Patti, then me. I was halfway through rinsing my hair when the water went from lukewarm to icy cold. Ever try to rinse out conditioner in cold water? After me it was Kate's turn.

I combed my hair down as flat as I could, put it in a ponytail, and hoped for the best. I decided to pretend to be sleeping when Kate came out of the bathroom, so that she couldn't discuss all the weird

74

happenings. If she sat there calmly going over all the "facts," I'd just scream!

There was no pretending necessary. I thought I was going to have a hard time falling asleep. But the minute I crawled into my sleeping bag, after shaking it one last time, I was history.

I was having a weird, complicated sort of dream. The boy we'd seen at the motel, the one with the interesting smile, had just dived into the creek, and I was trying to warn him: "Not the creek! The creek is the lair of a dangerous — "

— then I woke up enough to realize that somebody was actually whispering, "The creek!"

I opened my eyes to find Patti and Lauren in Kate's and my room, sitting on Kate's bed. At least I guessed it was Patti and Lauren — it was really dark, so all I could make out were three lumps sitting on Kate's bed.

I glanced at my watch, which has hands that glow in the dark: one-fifteen. "What's going on?" I asked drowsily.

"Patti thinks she saw a light outside," Kate whispered.

"Where outside?" I said, the hair starting to stand up on the back of my neck.

"Toward the creek," Patti whispered.

The creek! I practically rocketed out of my sleeping bag. "Let's tell Nick and Tara!"

"No, I don't want to bother them yet," Patti said softly.

"Patti thinks she might have been dreaming," Kate said. "Dreaming about the burglars. We're going into Patti and Lauren's room to keep watch for a while."

"Well, don't leave me here!" I shrieked.

So the four of us crept across the hall and sat down in a row on Patti's bed, right next to the window.

The moon was just a sliver, hanging low in the sky. There were clouds across the stars, so it was absolutely black out there. I felt as if I had never really seen just how black and spooky a night could be. *If I were at home,* I thought, *I would be tucked into my own bed with no bugs, and my parents would be just down the hall. I'd be completely safe. . . .*

"What did the light look like?" I whispered to Patti. "The one in your . . . dream?"

"It was sort of a — a green glow," Patti said. I heard Lauren catch her breath. "Low to the ground and mostly hidden by trees." I scooted so close to Patti that I was practically sitting in her lap. All four of us crowded closer together, and peered silently through the window.

Nothing happened for ages. Kate dozed off and slipped sideways, until her head ended up resting on my back. Then she started to snore. Trust Kate to be so calm in the face of disaster.

Patti, Lauren, and I hummed a few choruses of the B29s' song, "Kick Out the Jams," to stay awake. I looked at my watch at five till two. And again at two-ten, and two-twenty.

The three of us started to nod. Patti muffled a yawn. "I guess I dreamed it after all," she said. "Let's go to bed."

"Yeah, the sky is getting lighter — it must be almost sunrise," Lauren mumbled sleepily.

"It can't be sunrise," I said, checking my watch for the hundredth time. "It's only two-thirty." Uh-oh . . . if it wasn't sunrise . . .

The three of us were suddenly wide awake, sitting straight up and leaning closer to the window to stare through the screen. Kate's head slipped off my back, and she toppled over onto the bed with a thump, but she didn't wake up.

"It's getting brighter," Lauren barely whispered.

Before, the trees had been a blacker line against the black sky. Now we could see the outlines of their shapes . . . because there was a dim light shining somewhere among them.

"Greenish," Patti whispered. "Doesn't it look sort of greenish?"

It was a yellowish-green hazy glow, and it was gliding smoothly through the trees.

"I think it's getting closer," Patti murmured. "If someone were carrying the light on foot, wouldn't it be bouncing up and down with every step?"

"What if they were swimming?" I couldn't help blurting out.

Lauren cracked first. "It's the burglars coming back! Or maybe it really is — " her voice choked — "the ghost!" she squeaked.

Kate sat up, suddenly wide awake. "Oh, Lauren, please!" she said. "Will you put this ghost stuff out of your head?" She reached over and impatiently flipped on the lamp next to the bed so she could frown at Lauren.

"Turn off the lamp, Kate!" Patti whispered urgently.

Kate snapped it off. But it was too late. The greenish-yellow light in the jungle had disappeared as quickly and completely as though it had been switched off as well.

"It's gone!" I said. "The light's gone."

Chapter 9

Kate and I woke up the next morning to the slam of a car door out front. A loud, cheerful voice was saying, ''All I'm asking is that you keep me in mind when you get ready to sell. There are major problems with the property, of course. But part of it is waterfront, so I might be able . . .''

''Who's that?'' Kate whispered to me.

''I told you before, we have no plans to sell this property, Mr. Grandy,'' Tara's voice said firmly.

''Well, I happened to run into Mayor Ellis yesterday, and I mentioned your idea about giving the property to the town. I have to tell you, he was not enthusiastic,'' Mr. Grandy said.

''I'll bet he wasn't, not by the time *you* got through with him,'' Kate muttered.

''Sssh!'' I said, still listening.

"The town doesn't have the funds that would be necessary to clear away the mess of brush around the creek," Mr. Grandy went on. "Or fix this house up as park headquarters, or a refreshment stand. And then there's the ghost business — "

"Surely you don't believe in ghosts, Mr. Grandy?" Tara said sharply.

"*I* might not, but a lot of taxpayers do," he replied.

"What does *that* mean?" I whispered to Kate.

"It means that the people who live in Puerto Delfin wouldn't want to spend their tax money fixing up a place that's haunted," Kate said. "What a creep!"

"Mr. Grandy," Tara began, her voice rising.

"I just felt you should know the facts," Greg Grandy interrupted. "I'll drop by later in the week."

As he started his car, Kate and I jumped out of our sleeping bags. "Who cares what he says?" Kate said. "Once the right people hear about the manatees, there will be plenty of interest in Aunt Mary's property, believe me!"

Kate offered me her lime-green baggy shorts and a pale pink polo shirt. Not exactly my style, but what could I do? "Thanks, Kate," I said.

We went out to the kitchen as Tara was coming in from the front. When she saw us, she wiped the frown off her face and smiled determinedly. "Good morning, girls. At least I hope *this* morning is going to be better than yesterday was!"

We smiled back at her. Things *did* look a lot better this morning. The sun was shining, and the house was starting to look more homey.

"Nick drove into town to call The Colonial Motel again about Stephanie's suitcase," Tara said. Now there's a nice guy! "But I have to tell you, Stephanie — I like you in pastels. And I like your hair curly, too."

"Curly" didn't begin to describe what my hair was like. I mean, I was scared to take it out of the ponytail, for fear of an explosion. But it was nice of her to say she liked it.

Tara made breakfast on Aunt Mary's old black metal stove: cornbread muffins, bacon, and eggs. Patti and Lauren wandered in just in time to eat it.

We spent most of the time talking about our newfound manatee. It seemed like the manatee was the *only* good thing that had happened since we had left Riverhurst.

"Exactly what *is* a manatee?" Kate asked.

"Scientists think they're distant cousins of elephants," Tara said knowledgeably.

"How large was the one you saw, do you think?" Patti asked.

"About the size of an average person," I said. "Right, Lauren?"

She nodded. "Only plump."

"Then he's not much more than a baby," Patti told us. "Adult manatees can weigh as much as two thousand pounds."

"Wow!" Lauren said.

"If I'd seen something that weird-looking weighing two thousand pounds, I would have fainted and fallen straight into the creek," said Kate. "It could have eaten me for supper."

Tara shook her head. "It might have swum over for a closer look, but manatees are vegetarians, and very gentle," she said.

"A baby," I said thoughtfully. "Does that mean his mother's hanging around there somewhere, too?"

"Probably. Mothers and babies stay together for as long as two years," Patti said. "At two years, the baby would be a lot larger than the one you saw."

Patti had learned about manatees in the Quarks Club back at Riverhurst Elementary, where the kids had been studying them, along with dolphins and whales. "Manatees hate cold water, and search out hot springs to hang around. The fact that you saw a manatee in Aunt Mary's creek could mean there's a hot spring flowing into it at some point."

Tara nodded. "When they're dozing, they only have to come to the surface to breathe every fifteen minutes or so," she said. "Normally, though, they surface about every couple of minutes. That must have been the sighs you heard, Stephanie."

"I'm so glad I didn't imagine the whole thing," I murmured.

"Me, too," Lauren said pointedly, looking at Kate.

"Okay, okay," Kate agreed. "So for once your imagination *wasn't* running away with you!" We all laughed.

Patti added, "*Anybody* seeing a manatee for the first time would believe they were imagining things. In the old days, sailors thought that manatees were mermaids."

"Not very pretty ones," Lauren said with a giggle. "Two-thousand-pounders with whiskers!"

"The important thing is there are fewer than a thousand of them left in the whole United States," Tara said, picking up her plate and carrying it to the sink.

"Now it's even more important that Aunt Mary's land be made into a permanent wildlife preserve," Patti pointed out.

"What if the mayor of Puerto Delfin won't go for it?" I asked.

"Then Uncle Nick and Tara will have to talk to the State Parks Department, or even the National Parks Department," Patti said. "These animals are seriously endangered!"

"Hey, what about the light we saw last night?"

Lauren asked. "Do manatees glow in the dark?"

"What light?" Tara asked, turning around at the sink.

"We saw a light in the woods last night," Kate explained calmly. "We watched it for a while from Patti's room, but nothing happened. It finally just went away."

When you turned on our light, I thought to myself.

Tara suddenly looked a lot less cheerful. "What now?" she sighed.

"I've been thinking," Patti said. "It was probably just swamp gas. You know — plants that rot in a swamp can give off a gas that's kind of fluorescent, right, Tara?"

Tara smiled weakly and nodded. "That's true. Maybe it was." But she didn't sound convinced.

Just then Uncle Nick hurried into the house, with good news and bad news. "The good news is, The Colonial Motel put Stephanie's suitcase on the bus to Jacksonville," he said. "We should have it tomorrow. Although I like you in this outfit, Stephanie — very vacationish."

I smiled at him. Everyone was being so nice about my missing suitcase. After all, it really was my own fault.

"Now for the bad news," Uncle Nick went on. "First, none of Aunt Mary's furniture has turned up in the antique stores in Puerto Delfin. Sheriff Gunn and I went to a couple of them just now, with no luck. But he'll be checking the ones in the neighboring towns. I also visited the mayor's office, and Mayor Ellis says he can't really consider taking on such a big responsibility as the upkeep of Aunt Mary's property, Tara." Then his face split into a big smile. "*But*, when he finds out about our manatees, I bet he'll be singing a different tune!"

"You didn't tell him, then?" Kate asked.

"No," Uncle Nick said. "I wanted to get in touch with my friend Warren first, and get some solid information. When we're really sure of what we have, we'll go back to the mayor, and Tara can convince them to set up the preserve."

"That's great, Nick," Tara said smiling. "We have some news, too. Patti thinks the manatee is just a baby, judging from Stephanie and Lauren's description. So we might have his mother in our creek, too. And, the girls saw someone with a light in the woods last night." I guess Tara hadn't bought the swamp gas explanation.

Uncle Nick looked amazed. "What is it with this place, honey?" he asked Tara. "Did Aunt Mary have a fortune buried here or what?"

Tara smiled and playfully hit his arm. "Not that I know of. But let's all be careful when we're outside, and no wandering off alone, girls. Now," she said, and her tone brightened, "let's drive into town and make some phone calls to Nick's friend. And we'll buy you a bathing suit at the same time, Stephanie. Something you can wear to snorkel in."

Bathing suit, yes, I thought. *Snorkeling, no.* If there were one-ton manatees in our little creek, I could only imagine what could be swimming around in the Gulf of Mexico.

After breakfast we washed up, then piled into the van to head for Puerto Delfin. Tara was driving, and Uncle Nick turned around to tell us about something funny he'd seen that morning.

"While the sheriff and I were talking to the owner of one of the antique stores, a couple drove up in a beat-up camper and asked him if he had any old bathtubs for sale. They bought two huge ones, and stuffed them side by side into their camper." Uncle Nick grinned and shook his head. "I don't know how they're going to move around back there now. They're going to have to *sleep* in the tubs."

"Two bathtubs in a camper? They must be the cleanest people in the world." Tara laughed.

"Actually, they were sort of messy-looking," Uncle Nick said. "The woman had hair flying every whichway, and the man wore a dirty shirt and had a cigar."

"It sounds like the Goodwins!" Kate said.

"Who?" said Nick.

86

"Mr. and Mrs. Goodwin. They were fishing on our beach yesterday afternoon," Tara told him. "Maybe they're going to keep their catch alive in those tubs."

Uncle Nick shrugged. "Two bathtubs full is an awful lot of fish," he said. "Unless they're selling the fish out of their camper."

Tara turned into a parking space on Front Street. "There's a pay phone, next to that clothing store, Beauty and the Beach." She turned the engine off and smiled. "It looks just right, doesn't it, girls?"

We piled out onto the sidewalk. Uncle Nick went to call his friend about our manatees, and we headed for the store with Tara. It was really nice to be back in civilization, I realized, with lots of people around. I felt myself relaxing for the first time in what seemed like a very long time. It was just so creepy being out in the woods with strangers sneaking around, weird lights, and no phone. . . . I shivered, in spite of the warm sun.

Beauty and the Beach was a great store. Not only did it carry bathing suits and beach stuff, like boogie boards, but it also sold regular clothes for kids, like T-shirts, pants, shorts, and crop tops. The only problem was, hardly anything was red or black.

The salesperson shook her head. "But, dear, black isn't very cheerful, is it? How about purple?" She held up a purple-and-black tiger-striped tank suit in front of me, and turned me around so I could see it in the full-length mirror.

"Cool!" said Patti.

"Go for it!" Lauren agreed.

"Be flexible, Stephanie," Kate advised.

I took a good look at the suit, and myself, and nodded. "I'll take this one." It *was* a pretty neat suit.

We all had money from our parents to spend on vacation souvenirs, and what's a better souvenir than something to wear? So we tried on clothes for about half an hour. Lauren ended up buying an orange sweatshirt, Kate bought a new pair of sunglasses, and Patti got a beaded African bracelet. Tara also bought me a pair of white shorts and a red T-shirt with FLORIDA written on it in puffy letters.

We paid for our stuff, and then Uncle Nick was outside, tapping on the glass door for us to come out. "I reached my friend in Washington," he reported as soon as we'd stepped outside. He lowered his voice. "Warren said to keep the manatee a secret for now. They're very timid, and the last thing we need is a crowd of people tramping along the creek, or worse, roaring up and down it in motorboats."

"Good morning, Ms. Chipley, Mr. Pollard, girls!" Greg Grandy, cheery as ever, practically bowed to us and strolled by. "A fabulous Florida day to you!"

Tara groaned softly. "I'm beginning to think that

man is following us," she said as we climbed into the van to hear what else Warren had told Uncle Nick. "He's determined to wear us down."

"Warren suggested that we get over to Wonderworld as soon as possible," Uncle Nick continued. We all cheered from the backseat. Way to go, Warren!

"What does Wonderworld have to do with our manatee, Uncle Nick?" Patti asked.

"There are three manatees living in captivity at Wonderworld, and they have a resident scientist who's a manatee expert," Uncle Nick said. "So I thought we might drive over there tomorrow."

"Yay!" we cheered again. "All right!"

"In the meantime, Warren said we should try to photograph our manatee," Uncle Nick added.

"What about videotaping it?" Kate asked.

"Even better," Tara said. "We'll take the tape with us to Wonderworld to show the expert."

We drove back home, and Uncle Nick fixed us peanut butter sandwiches for lunch. Then Tara made us wait for an hour while our food settled. Finally, we changed into our bathing suits, and I wore my new shorts and T-shirt over mine. Then, we slathered quarts of Bugaway on our arms and legs, and Tara stuffed towels and our snorkeling gear into a big straw bag.

It was almost one-thirty, a lot earlier in the afternoon than it had been when Tara and the four of us had walked into the jungle the day before. It seemed at least twice as hot.

"That water is going to feel so good," Kate said, wiping beads of sweat away from her forehead. I had to agree. I had never felt such sticky, muggy air. I couldn't wait to dive into that lovely Gulf water.

As usual, mosquitoes were buzzing all around us, and it was hard to swat them away. The Bugaway was working pretty well, though. I felt a little nervous being in these woods again. But I reminded myself that Uncle Nick was with us, and Tara had waved her machete pretty fiercely at that stranger yesterday. Between Uncle Nick and her, I figured we were safe.

We struggled through the bushes until we reached the spot where Lauren and I had spotted the baby manatee. Then we hunkered down on the creek bank to wait for him to reappear. On the drive back to the house we had discussed what to name the baby manatee. We had finally decided on "Tug," after Tug Keeler, who's a quarterback for Riverhurst High. They *do* look a whole lot alike.

While we were sitting on the bank, we saw a couple of turtles, followed by what Uncle Nick said was a "common water rat." It looked *un*commonly huge to me and Kate. We both jumped to our feet, and since there was nothing handy to climb on, we stood on our tiptoes and hoped for the best.

Tara wasn't crazy about the rat, either. Or the mosquitoes. "Nick, I think the girls and I will try the reef for a while, okay?" she said.

"Go ahead," said Uncle Nick. He pulled his cap down lower on his forehead, and waved the video camera at us. "I'm tough, I can take it," he said with a grin. "I'll catch up with you in a little while."

What a difference, stepping out of that buggy steambath into the cool ocean breeze. The beach was absolutely empty again. We spread out our towels and peeled off our sneakers, shorts, and shirts. But when Tara started handing out the snorkeling gear, I shook my head.

"No, thanks," I said. "I think I'll sit this one out, work on my tan, maybe pick up some more shells. . . ."

"But this is going to be great, Stephanie!" Lauren insisted.

"You don't want to miss our first time on the reef!" Patti chimed in.

"Besides, you need this as a dress rehearsal for next time, when we'll tape it," said Kate over her shoulder. The three of them were already waddling toward the Gulf in their flippers, like large mutant ducks.

Tara smiled at me understandingly. "Give it a

try. The tide's going out, so the water should be pretty shallow. I'll keep an eye out for any unwanted underwater visitors, I promise. It's going to get awfully hot out here,'' she added.

The sun *was* really scorching — even my hair was hot!

"Well . . . okay," I said. As long as Tara would be on guard . . . I pulled on my own flippers and mask, and walked with her down to the water.

The top of the coral reef was only about four feet underwater at low tide. It looked like a narrow ridge of white rock, but it wasn't. Tara told us it's actually made up of skeletons left behind by zillions of tiny sea animals called polyps.

Swirling around the reef were huge schools of fish of all different kinds: small, sleek silver ones; plump, pinkish oval ones; flat green ones. My favorites had long, swoopy tails and black-and-white stripes.

Transparent shrimp paraded around on the reef itself, which was decorated with spiny sea urchins in purple and hot pink, bright yellow sponges, and sea cucumbers, which look like smaller versions of The Blob, and are animals, not vegetables.

As I said earlier, I really wasn't enthusiastic about sharing the reef with large and dangerous sea creatures. Or about wrinkling my skin up like a prune's, or swimming around with a hose sticking out of my mouth, looking like a major geek. But the reef was so beautiful that I actually forgot about those drawbacks.

After a while, Kate and I started to get tired. We paddled back to the beach to sack out on our towels for a while in the sun, while Tara, Patti, and Lauren did some more underwater exploring.

I guess I'd dozed off, because the next thing I heard was an awful rattling sound practically on top of me. I sat up quickly, about to leap off my towel, but Kate grabbed my arm and giggled, "It's okay — it's just the Goodwins." The rattling stopped, because the Goodwins had parked on the beach just about twenty-five feet from us.

"Still here?" Mrs. Goodwin called. Mr. Goodwin just grunted — he was baiting the hooks on several fishing poles.

"I guess you haven't seen any ghosts, yet," Mrs. Goodwin went on.

No, I thought. *Just bugs, manatees, cut wires, and weird lights at night. . . .*

Kate must have been thinking along the same lines. "No ghosts — just green lights," she called back.

"Green lights? When was that?" Mrs. Goodwin asked sharply.

"Last night," Kate said. "Late."

"We thought maybe it was swamp gas," I

added, to see if Mrs. Goodwin would agree.

Just then, Tara, Patti, and Lauren swam in from the reef, babbling about the fish and the gorgeous colors and everything else, so Mrs. Goodwin didn't say anything more.

Finally Tara said, "We'd better rescue Nick, before the mosquitoes swallow him alive."

We decided to follow the creek back, which meant trudging past the Goodwins and their rusty camper. Kate and I were sort of straggling along, the last of our group. When we got even with the camper, what Uncle Nick had said about the two old bathtubs popped into our heads.

"They're busy fishing, anyway," Kate murmured. "They won't notice us taking a quick look."

We hopped up onto the running board on the driver's side, and peered through a dusty little window. Sure enough, there were two large bathtubs stuffed into their camper, and I mean stuffed!

"How in the world do they move around in there?" Kate was saying, when Lauren stopped and looked back for us. "Kate! Stephanie!" she called softly, and motioned wildly.

"Just a second!" we mouthed back. There wasn't much else in the camper in the way of furniture, just a big pile of what looked like fishing net at the front end, and a couple of narrow bunks.

"Stephanie!" Lauren insisted.

Suddenly a loud voice snarled, "What are you kids up to, snooping around private property?!"

It was Mrs. Goodwin, back for more bait. She looked even less friendly than she had before. In fact, she was positively scowling as she strode quickly toward us.

My sneakered feet slipped off the running board onto the sand. Kate and I backed away from the camper as fast as we could.

"Uh . . . n-nothing!" I stammered. Mrs. Goodwin looked so angry, for a minute I thought she might come grab us or something!

Then Tara turned around at the edge of the trees and yelled over the crash of the surf, "Everything okay back there? Are you guys coming?"

"You bet!" Kate yelled back.

Mrs. Goodwin ground to a halt, gave Kate and me one last angry glare, then turned away to look unsmilingly at Tara. Kate and I ran across the sand to catch up with the others. Finally we reached them, panting, and Lauren said, "What was that all about?"

"I don't know. We just wanted to look at the bathtubs. But Mrs. Goodwin got really angry about it," Kate said, "almost as if she were trying to hide something."

Chapter
10

We followed the path and met up with Uncle Nick again. He was still crouched down next to the creek. He looked hot, tired, sweaty, and a little mosquito-bitten, but he was absolutely beaming!

"Tug is still here!" he exclaimed as soon as he saw us. "I think I got a pretty good shot of him with the video camera. He surfaced right in front of that cypress stump, took a deep breath, caught a glimpse of me, and disappeared. No sign of an older manatee, though." Uncle Nick shook his head and looked a little worried. "If Tug is an orphan, we're in trouble."

"We'll talk to the experts at Wonderworld first thing tomorrow morning," Tara said. "They'll tell us what to do."

Our video camera has one of those tiny viewing screens on it, so you can check out what you've filmed without waiting to use a VCR. We looked at

Uncle Nick's tape when we got back to the house, and there was Tug, about the size of a match head, blinking at us.

"Isn't he adorable?" Tara said. "I think the name you chose for him is perfect, girls. I can just imagine him in a football uniform."

For the rest of the afternoon Patti, Lauren, Kate, and I decided to just hang out — we were pretty tired from being up half the night before. Kate helped Tara organize the kitchen cabinets (she was in heaven), and Lauren bunked down to take a nap. Patti and I went out onto the screened porch and read — I had brought the latest *Marlo James, Fashion Model* book.

Later we all got together and decided what we were going to wear to Wonderworld. I ended up borrowing a pair of plaid walking shorts from Lauren, and Patti's pink and white pullover. There was nothing I could do about my red sneakers clashing, though, because we all have different-sized feet.

Then we strung shell necklaces for a while with the yarn we had picked up in Puerto Delfin that morning. We made some for ourselves, and for Hope Lenski, Jane Sykes, Robin Becker, and some of the other girls back at Riverhurst Elementary.

Before dinner we helped Tara pile up old newspapers and magazines and other trash to take to the dump later in the week. Then we had grilled hamburgers outside.

Even though it had been a great day, I couldn't help feeling a little worried as Kate and I were getting ready for bed. As we shook out our sleeping bags, I asked, "Do you really think it's okay for us to stay here? What would our parents say if they knew about the intruder in the woods, and the cut wires, and the burglars. . . ." I trailed off. I didn't want Kate to think I was a big baby, but I couldn't help feeling a little scared.

"Well," Kate said, "I think we're okay. After all, we have Uncle Nick and Tara with us and the house is locked up tight at night. And Sheriff Gunn said he'd be keeping an eye on the place." I nodded. When she put it that way, I felt a little better. For once, I was glad that Kate was so practical and certain about things.

Patti and Lauren tapped on our door to say goodnight.

"Let's try not to have any more midnight scares, okay?" Lauren said. I could tell she was only half-joking. "After all, we have to hit the road by seven tomorrow. Wonderworld opens at nine o'clock — and we don't want to miss a single wonderful second!"

And we didn't. We were right near the front of the line when the huge clock on the Wonderworld

Castle bonged nine times, and the iron gates to the theme park slowly swung open.

"Can you believe the size of that roller coaster?" Kate exclaimed. "It's taller than the First National Bank building back home!"

"Look at the waterfall!" Patti said. "And that old Viking ship!"

"I want to go on every ride in the park," Lauren said, starting to list them, "The Water Slide, The Sky Diver, The Submariner, The Haunted House. . . ."

"The Haunted House! Are you kidding me?" I squawked, and everyone laughed.

"Spaceflight to Pluto, Journey to the Earth's Core," Patti continued.

"Swashbuckling Adventures from the Silver Screen, The Cliff-hanger Railroad," Kate added.

"What about all these boutiques?" I pointed out. "We're surrounded with shopping possibilities. Shoes and sweaters from Italy, jeans and tops from France, jackets from Japan!"

Uncle Nick and Tara burst out laughing. "You'll all have your chance," Tara promised.

"But can you hold off for just a couple of minutes while I try to make an appointment with the manatee expert? I'll be back in a flash," Uncle Nick said.

While Kate, Lauren, Patti, and I had a friendly disagreement about what we should do first, Uncle

Nick sprinted over to a redbrick building not far from the gates. It had a sign on it that said ADMINISTRATION. By the time the four of us had decided that it might make the most sense to split up, he was back.

"She'll see us at three o'clock this afternoon," he told Tara. "Ms. Balcom is her name, and I left the videotape for her to study in the meantime."

"The girls want to break up into two groups," Tara told him. "I think that's all right, don't you?"

"Sure," Uncle Nick said. "This park is as safe as our backyard."

"Safer, probably," I murmured.

Tara checked her watch. "Why don't we meet right here to have lunch together at twelve-thirty?"

"Excellent!" the four of us chorused.

So Tara and Uncle Nick headed for the two-hundred-acre Wonderworld Zoo, Patti and Kate planned to ride The Cliff-hanger Railroad, and then fly to Pluto, and Lauren and I made an agreement to take turns, too: one of Lauren's rides, and one of my shops.

She and I were standing next to a row of phone booths, trying to make up our minds which to do first, ride or shop, when we heard a voice beside us say, "Yes, that's right! We've found them! And they're gorgeous. What? No — I don't think so. It shouldn't be any problem to get them back home. We'll just have to be careful and keep it quiet."

100

I looked at Lauren and raised one eyebrow. We leaned over and peered around the edge of the phone booth. It was her! The cute boy's mom, the one we had seen at the Galley-Ho, and then again at The Colonial Motel.

"Is she talking about dolphins again?" Lauren whispered.

We both strained our ears to listen.

"Yes, I know they're endangered. That's why they're so valuable. And if they're healthy, they're worth a lot more than that."

"What's she talking about?" I hissed into Lauren's ear.

"I don't know, but it sounds pretty suspicious," Lauren whispered back.

"Okay," the woman was saying. She gave a short laugh. "Well, we'll just have to steal them away, that's all. I'll make them an offer they can't refuse. . . ."

Lauren and I stared at each other, our eyes round. Then we heard the woman hang up, and we dashed around the corner of a Hawaiian souvenir shop. We peered around and saw her head off in the opposite direction.

"Whoa," Lauren said. "What a weird conversation."

"Oh, it probably wasn't what it sounded like," I said uncertainly.

That's when somebody said, "Hey," in a friendly sort of way.

Lauren and I whirled around to find ourselves face-to-face with the really cute boy! The mysterious woman's son! Two days ago I would have given anything to meet him, but now his turning up just seemed to confuse everything.

But the boy didn't seem to notice our surprise. He just grinned at us with that cute, lopsided grin, and said, "Haven't I seen you somewhere before?"

Lauren and I nodded, still speechless, and the boy added, "I'm Josh — Josh Marcus." He was wearing khakis and a gray jersey the color of his eyes. His hair was combed a little to one side, and it was blonder than I'd remembered.

I found my voice first. "Hi," I said. "I'm Stephanie Green, and this is Lauren Hunter."

"We seem to keep running into each other," Josh said. "Are you staying at the hotel here at the park?"

"No, we drove over from Puerto Delfin," Lauren said.

"Oh, I know where that is," Josh said. "My family and I drove through there yesterday. It's a pretty town."

"Our friend Patti's aunt and uncle have a house there," I explained. "Are you staying here?"

"One more day — then we're heading down to

the Keys, I guess," Josh said. "My mom and dad want to go skin diving, and do some underwater photography. They're, uh, really interested in sea mammals," he continued awkwardly.

My eyes met Lauren's. Were Josh's parents interested enough in sea mammals to *steal* them? It was such a strange coincidence that Josh's family would have driven through Puerto Delfin. After all, it's such a small town, and kind of off the beaten path.

Lauren must have decided to find out more, because she said, "Really? Did you see the fantastic coral reef in Puerto Delfin? We snorkeled there yesterday. It's great because it's only about six feet down."

"Depth isn't too much of a problem," Josh said. "We all have scuba gear. But, no, we didn't see the reef. We just passed through." He sort of blushed and looked away. Was it my imagination, or was Josh hiding something?

If Josh did scuba diving, it meant he was older than we were, twelve at least, which is the minimum age for a scuba permit.

"So, where are you guys headed?" Josh asked.

"The Submariner," I said without thinking.

"Oh? Mind if I hang out with you for a while?" he asked politely.

"Uh, Stephanie, could I see you for a moment?" Lauren asked, pulling at my arm. I shrugged and made an apologetic face at Josh while Lauren led me a couple of feet away.

"What's up?" I whispered.

"I think we should hang out with Josh for a while — you know, to see if we can find out what's going on with his mom," Lauren said in a low voice.

"Sounds good to me. We'll just have to try to act normal, though. And for goodness' sake, don't say anything about Tug!"

Lauren nodded, and we went back over to Josh. I smiled at him. I couldn't help thinking that while his parents might be criminals, he seemed awfully nice. And cute.

"Sure, let's go!" I said as cheerfully as I could.

"What about your, um, family?" Lauren asked as we walked to our next ride.

"My brother and I are supposed to meet our mom and dad in front of the Italian Pavilion for lunch at twelve-thirty. So we have almost two hours. Let's have some fun," Josh said, giving us his great smile again.

We got to the entrance of the Submariner and stood in line. Then we climbed down an iron ladder into a narrow room with metal walls covered with all sorts of controls and lights and dials.

"I went aboard a real sub once," Josh told us. "This is a lot like the real thing." My eyes met Lauren's again. Why would a twelve-year-old have gone on a submarine?

We strapped ourselves into our seats, and an engine rumbled to life somewhere behind us. Suddenly the sub went into a crash dive. Little round windows sprang open in the hull in front of us, and we were staring out at a rocky underwater cliff, with all sorts of exotic fish swimming around. It was completely realistic.

The fish got larger and weirder as the sub dived farther into the depths. Suddenly, a huge pink tentacle stretched across the windows! It wrapped around the submarine, and shook it like a toy!

"A giant squid!" Lauren and I couldn't help screaming as the squid peered in at us with its evil yellow eyes. Okay, I know Patti told us it probably would never happen in real life. But even Josh yelled, and hung onto his seat!

The squid dragged the submarine farther down into the depths. Just when we thought our sub was doomed, an even more gigantic killer whale swooshed past the windows in our hull. He and the squid had a battle to the death right in front of us. The whale won — it was awesome.

When the ride was over, we unbuckled ourselves and crawled back up the ladder into the Florida sunshine. We decided to go on the roller coaster next.

"So, Josh," I said casually as we walked along, "is your school on spring break now?"

"Yeah. My parents decided to come over to Florida on a kind of working vacation," Josh said.

"Oh? What do your parents do?" Lauren came right out and asked. I held my breath and waited.

"Wow! Look at that!" Josh said, pointing to the big arch of the roller coaster, which was right in front of us. "This looks great! Come on!" Josh ran and got in line, motioning for us to follow him.

"Do you get the feeling he doesn't want to talk about his parents?" I asked Lauren.

"Yep," Lauren said grimly. We went and got in line with our mystery boy.

Josh, Lauren, and I went on some other rides, too, like the water slide — 750 feet long — where all three of us got absolutely soaked. We hadn't had much of a chance to ask Josh more questions while we were on the roller coaster or the water slide, so I suggested that we go on the world's largest Ferris wheel and give our clothes a chance to dry off.

It was great. We could see the entire park from the top, including the zoo and the dolphin and seal pools — which got me to thinking. Dolphins and seals are both sea mammals. So are manatees. If Josh's mom didn't want dolphins, was she planning to steal seals or manatees right here from Wonderworld?!

"Ohmygosh!" I gasped, stunned by that thought. Josh and Lauren both looked up quickly.

"Are you okay, Stephanie?" Josh asked. "We *are* up pretty high."

"Oh, no, I'm okay," I said, trying to laugh. "No problem."

I could feel Lauren staring at me, wondering what was wrong. But I had to just sit there. Josh was chatting easily, and he mentioned that he's from San Diego, California. Which meant that there was no way I'd ever see him again. . . .

Stephanie! I scolded myself. *You don't want to see this guy again, anyway. No matter how cute he is! His parents might be crooks!*

By the time we'd finished riding the Ferris wheel, it was almost twelve-thirty, time for Josh to go to lunch with his parents, and for us to meet Uncle Nick and Tara.

Chapter
11

"You guys have a couple of minutes, right? Why don't you come meet my folks? They'd like to hear about the reef in Puerto Delfin that we missed," Josh suggested as we hurried toward the Italian Pavilion.

I almost stopped in my tracks. The thought of meeting a possible criminal face-to-face scared me. But we were supposed to meet Uncle Nick and Tara close by anyway.

Lauren must have decided the same thing, because she said, "Okay. Fine."

Then Josh waved to a man and woman wearing purple and white Wonderworld caps who were standing near the entrance to the Italian Pavilion restaurant. "There are my mom and dad." *It's funny how normal they look,* I thought. Just like anybody else's parents. Not like criminals at all. All the same, I was really glad that we hadn't told Josh about our manatee, and the real reason we were here at Wonderworld.

But as it turned out, Uncle Nick and Tara spilled the beans themselves.

Josh introduced us to his parents. He told them about the reef in Puerto Delfin and their eyes lit up.

"Really?" Josh's mom said. "That's fascinating. I didn't know about it." *She seems so nice,* I thought sadly. What had made her turn to a life of crime? Just then Uncle Nick and Tara showed up, on their way to our gathering point near the front gates.

Practically the first words out of their mouths after hellos all around were about the manatees. I almost slapped my hand against my forehead. So much for keeping our big secret.

"They have two female manatees in a big tank next door to the zoo," Tara told us. "And a baby not much larger than Tug."

"Who is Tug?" Mrs. Marcus asked.

So Tara and Nick filled the Marcuses in on the manatee in our creek. I watched Mrs. Marcus carefully. She got more and more excited as Tara and Nick described how we had found him.

"Wild manatees? Right by your house?" She was practically jumping up and down! Lauren and I looked at each other and nodded. "But that's amazing! They're very scarce, you know. They've been endangered for a while."

"Yes, we know," Lauren said.

Mrs. Marcus looked at her husband. "Honey, I think we just can't miss this opportunity. . . ." Mr. Marcus nodded, then looked up at Uncle Nick and Tara. "We're very interested in sea mammals — all kinds," he said. "I think we're going to have to come to Puerto Delfin and take a look at your manatee."

"That would be lovely," Tara said, while inside I was thinking, *No! No! No!* But there was nothing I could do. I just had to watch helplessly as Tara gave the Marcuses our address. Now in addition to stealing manatees from Wonderworld, the Marcuses would try to capture ours!

Uncle Nick asked Josh to have lunch with us, and there was nothing we could do except plaster smiles onto our faces and nod. Josh arranged to meet up again with his family after we had our appointment with Ms. Balcom, the manatee expert.

"Great," Lauren whispered in my ear as we headed toward the gate to meet Patti and Kate. "Then he can go back and tell his parents exactly what Ms. Balcom says!"

I nodded. "We have to tell the others as soon as possible!" I whispered back.

I thought Kate's eyes were going to pop right out of her head when she spotted us walking toward the gate with Josh. But before we'd taken three more steps, she'd pulled the video camera out of her tote and was recording the whole thing on film for the Video Club. I'd forgotten about her dumb vacation movie! Normally I would have loved to be seen with a really cute boy, but not today, when I was so worried about what would happen to Tug now that the Marcuses knew about him.

"Kate, cut that out!" I hissed as soon as we were within earshot.

"If you'd told me we were going to be on camera, I'd have worn a nicer shirt," Josh said with a grin. Whatever his parents were or did, I had to admit that Josh was a really neat guy. He was cute, funny, and really easy to be around. It was too bad that I couldn't have met him under better circumstances.

We ate lunch at El Taco Grande, where we stuffed ourselves on Mexican food. We barely had time to finish before we rushed over to the dolphin pool to see the afternoon show.

It was fun, I guess. The dolphins did belly flops and backflips, danced on their tails to music, and shook flippers with little kids in the audience. But it kind of bothered me that the dolphins had to clown around in a tank, even if they did seem to be enjoying the applause.

Just as I was having those thoughts, Josh said, "They ought to be free, roaming the oceans, instead of penned up here, acting goofy." Josh and I were definitely on the same wavelength. Maybe he didn't know what his parents were up to. I couldn't blame *him* for what they were going to do. . . .

Next we visited the Great Barrier Reef, designed to look like the coral reef in Australia, in a 300,000-gallon aquarium of its own. It was amazing, with angelfish, butterfly fish, clown fish, and even some small stingrays and sharks swimming around.

I wasn't halfway through looking when Uncle Nick checked his watch and announced, "Ms. Balcom said she wanted to meet us at the manatee tank in about two minutes."

We hustled over and got there first, to discover all three manatees lying on the bottom of the pool. The pool had transparent plastic sides, so we could see them. Their faces looked just like Tug's — only bigger. Their bodies looked sort of like huge versions of the mushy sea cucumbers on the reef at Puerto Delfin. They also looked . . .

"Dead!" Kate said. "They look dead. Why aren't they moving?" The manatees were stretched out on their stomachs, with their short, thick flippers spread out from their sides. Their eyes were closed, and they weren't moving a muscle.

"Do you think they're okay?" Lauren asked Patti, as Ms. Balcom arrived. She was small and slender, with a dark tan from all the swimming she does in her job.

"They're absolutely fine, just napping," Ms. Balcom told us. "Manatees spend almost half of their day taking naps. See, now Miranda has an itch." Slowly but surely, one of the larger manatees rotated underwater to scratch her back on the bottom of the pool. Then the baby surfaced for a sighing breath of air.

"This baby, Hercules, is probably about the same age as your Tug — ten months," Ms. Balcom told us. "And I have some good news for you. On the video screen in the lab, your tape clearly shows the eyes and nose of an adult manatee, lurking close to a floating log. I'm pretty sure it's Tug's mother. Unlike dolphins, manatees in the wild are often timid around humans. The older they get, the more cautious they are, which is probably why you haven't gotten a good look at her."

"That's a huge relief," Tara said. "We didn't have a clue as to what to feed a baby manatee."

"Wow! Two manatees right in your own creek!" Josh said. So much for our secret — I didn't see how we could protect Tug and his mother anymore.

"When they get older, they're vegetarians like their parents," Ms. Balcom said. She pulled a head of regular lettuce out of a canvas bag and swished it around in the water of the pool. "Adult manatees will eat water weeds, algae, or even the sorts of things you might have in a salad." The manatee Ms. Balcom had called "Miranda" surfaced near us and plucked the head of lettuce daintily from her hand.

"What are those scars on her sides?" Josh asked. Miranda was covered with deep gouges — which had healed — running from one end of her body to the other.

"Those are propeller slashes," Ms. Balcom said. "Miranda wandered into a shipping channel by mistake, and a freighter accidentally ran over her. They called us, and a crane hoisted Miranda onto our truck — she weighs about fourteen hundred pounds. We started sewing her up and giving her antibiotics. Hercules is her baby. If she had died, he probably would have, too. If manatee babies are orphaned," Ms. Balcom went on, "it's essential to find them a foster mother quickly. Without manatee milk, they can't survive. And I have some more news for you," Ms. Balcom told Tara and Uncle Nick. "I made a few phone calls to conservationist groups around the state, and several of them are eager to talk to you about turning your property in Puerto Delfin into a permanent preserve for these big guys!"

"Excellent!" We all clapped.

"So we'll just have to make sure they're okay, and no one bothers them," I said, looking right at Josh. Josh just smiled and nodded at me. He sure knew how to play innocent!

"I know it's just what Aunt Mary would have wanted," Tara said a little tearfully.

"There was the business we mentioned to you," Uncle Nick said to Ms. Balcom in a lower voice. "The problem about ghosts?"

"A few ghostly visitors wouldn't bother the manatees," Ms. Balcom said with a smile.

"Ghosts?" Josh asked.

"It's a long story," Kate said, rolling her eyes.

Ms. Balcom asked Tara and Uncle Nick what day would be best for her to come up to the house and check out our manatees. They decided on Friday, three days away, since that was Ms. Balcom's day off from her job at Wonderworld.

Uncle Nick told us we had time for one more ride before we headed back to Puerto Delfin. Josh was still with us. We all agreed on The Swashbuckling Adventures from the Silver Screen, and swashbuckled our way through a pirate movie set on a pirate ship, a Western movie on a runaway stage coach, and a musketeer movie with sword fights and other fun stuff.

Then we finally said good-bye to Mr. and Mrs. Marcus and Josh, and I breathed a sigh of relief. The more I was getting to know Josh, the more I liked him. But I still didn't trust him or his parents.

Tara invited all the Marcuses for lunch the next day, after they checked into their rooms at Grandy's Grand Hotel. "I can't recommend the hotel personally," Tara said truthfully, "because I haven't been inside it in years. But it's the only one in town."

Nick said, "You probably won't be able to telephone us when you get there, because our phone isn't working. So we'll expect you when we see you."

"We'll just unpack, get settled, and drive on out to your house," Mrs. Marcus said. "It's at the end of Ocean Drive, right?"

"That's right," said Tara. "Through the wooden gate, up the dirt road to a small white house with a screened porch and yellow shutters. And be sure to bring your scuba equipment!"

"You bet!" said Mr. Marcus.

"See you tomorrow!" Mrs. Marcus said.

"See you guys tomorrow!" Josh repeated with his adorable smile. "I had a great time today."

"So did we," I said kind of sadly.

"Good-bye, Willie, hello, Josh," Kate sang under her breath as we walked out the front gates of Wonderworld. Wait till they heard what I *really* thought about Josh Marcus — and his family.

Chapter
12

It was late in the afternoon, and we were pretty tired by the time we started back toward Puerto Delfín. But Uncle Nick couldn't resist trying a new route. "Coming and going the same way?" He shook his head and opened a road map. "Too boring."

Which is how we found ourselves wandering around a little-known part of the state that we couldn't seem to locate on our road map. There were no motels, no fast-food places, not even any gas stations — just miles of two-lane highways that all appeared to end in one place: the Gulf of Mexico.

"Isn't that a great view?" said Uncle Nick for the fourth time as he pulled the minivan up to the end of a dead-end road, and we stared out at the sandy beach and blue water in front of us.

"Nick, this is getting ridiculous! We're going to turn around, drive back the way we came, and stop at the first building we see," Tara said firmly. "I don't care if it's somebody's house. I'm going inside to ask for directions."

"You're the boss," Uncle Nick said, putting the van into reverse. But I could tell he thought that actually asking for directions sort of ruined the game.

Anyway, the first building we came to was a small, two-story house on the edge of a tiny town named — it's the truth — Hoopin' Holler. It looked like a regular house, but there was a sign in the window that said, ANTIQUES BARN AT REAR.

"Everybody stay where you are," Tara ordered. I was too tired to move, anyway. I was just going over all the weird happenings of this trip — and wondering what Lauren and I would tell the others about Josh.

Tara hurried up the sidewalk and knocked on the front door of the house. When nobody answered, she walked around back to a big red barn with white trim, and disappeared inside.

"I wouldn't have thought we needed that many directions," Uncle Nick said after five minutes had passed and she still wasn't back. "Just 'turn left' or 'turn right.' I think I'll go see what's taking so long."

Patti, Kate, Lauren, and I figured we might as well join them. So we piled out of the car, and reached the door of the barn just in time to hear Tara saying, "Look, I know my own aunt's table when I see it!"

"There must have been thousands of tables like this one manufactured sixty or seventy years ago!" the angry, gray-haired owner said. He was lounging at a metal desk in the middle of the store, completely surrounded by old furniture.

The table they were talking about was close to the door. It was round and made of dark wood, about four feet across. It had wooden balls at the bottoms of its curved legs. I'd seen others like it myself — Nana used to have one in her kitchen.

Tara shook her head. "No, this is Aunt Mary's table. See that U-shaped dent in the top? That's where she dropped a big pitcher of lemonade."

The gray-haired man just rolled his eyes, and I could see his point, because anything could have made that dent.

"These scratches were left by Maude, Aunt Mary's cat," Tara said, pointing to some lighter-colored grooves in the trim on the side of the table.

The gray-haired man yawned and started rearranging some papers on his desk.

"All right, what about this?" Tara said triumphantly. "Look on the underside of the table. I carved my name — Tara — there one rainy morning when I couldn't play outside and I was bored."

Uncle Nick crouched down next to her to peer at one of the wooden balls at the bottom of the table. He grinned. "Yeah, what about this?" he said.

The man sighed impatiently, but he trudged over to take a look. "So?" he said.

"Well, what does this carving say?" Tara said evenly.

The gray-haired man bent over and squinted. "T-A-R-A . . . hey, listen, lady, I don't buy stolen furniture!" His tone had sure changed! "I got this from one of my regular suppliers," the man explained. "He drives down from northern Florida."

"What is his name?" Tara asked, ready to write it down in her little notebook.

"Uh, I don't know if I should give that out," the man said uncertainly.

"It doesn't really matter. I know where you are, and I know where the table is, and I'm sure the sheriff back in Puerto Delfin will be very interested," Tara said. "I guess we can count on you to keep an eye on this table for us? It's got a lot of sentimental value."

The man sighed. "Oh, okay — if you say so. Like I said, I didn't know it was stolen." He put a yellow SOLD tag on it. "There. Happy? It's not going anywhere."

We all turned and headed out the door.

"I didn't see the chairs, Nick," Tara said on our way back to the van. "Or the missing chest of draw-

120

ers. And he didn't seem to have any brass beds in the shop at all."

"His 'supplier' probably scattered them around the state," Uncle Nick said. "Anyway, we can buy other chairs. The main thing is, we've gotten Aunt Mary's table back, with your name on it."

"I'll never complain about your travels off the beaten track again!" Tara promised him.

Still, Tara did the driving from then on, and she turned in at the first gas station we passed to find out the quickest way back to Puerto Delfin. We made it to Front Street before it was completely dark outside.

As we rolled past Grandy's Grand, Uncle Nick suggested, "Why don't we take a quick look at the lobby, to make sure it's okay for the Marcuses."

"Good idea — you and the girls check out the hotel, and I'll run next door to the sheriff," Tara said. "Anndd" — she drew the word out importantly — "cross over to the bus station and pick up Stephanie's suitcase! It should be here from Ocala."

"Allll riight!" I said. It was funny, though — so much had been happening that I hadn't had time to worry about my clothes not matching perfectly, or whether or not my hair was too curly, or any of the stuff I usually worry about.

So Tara went to visit the sheriff, and Uncle Nick and the four of us climbed the steps up to the front door of Grandy's Grand and stepped inside.

121

"It's kind of nice," Patti said. And it was, in an old-fashioned sort of way. The lobby had ceiling fans, lots of comfortable wicker chairs, even a squawking green parrot in a huge cage in one corner.

"It's like that old black-and-white movie, *Slow Boat to Bali*," Kate said. "Neat!"

"At least Greg Grandy had the good sense not to change the style of the *inside* of this place," Uncle Nick said, satisfied with the lobby. "The Marcuses should be fine here."

But before we could make our escape, Greg Grandy himself was hurrying across the lobby toward us. "Mr. Pollard! Have you changed your mind about selling the property?" he said eagerly. "I was in your neighborhood this morning, and I stopped by the house. But no one was around, so I thought maybe you'd decided to cut your vacation short."

"Not at all," Uncle Nick interrupted. "We spent the day at Wonderworld. And my wife hasn't decided to sell. We just dropped by to take a look at the hotel."

Greg Grandy's round face fell. "Oh, really? Well, what about your . . . ghosts?" he lowered his voice almost to a whisper.

"Ghosts, shmosts," Uncle Nick replied pleasantly. "Come along, girls — Tara is probably waiting for us in the car."

"Ghosts, shmosts?" Kate repeated as we skipped

down the front steps. The five of us burst out laughing.

"I'm getting a little tired of Mr. Grandy throwing that in our faces every time we see him. Those rumors are a mighty convenient way to try to get Tara to sell the property cheaply," Uncle Nick said. "There she is now."

Sure enough, Tara was walking down the sidewalk toward us. "I reported the antique store owner in Hoopin' Holler to Sheriff Gunn. The sheriff's department down there will be paying him a visit first thing tomorrow morning. But, Stephanie, your suitcase didn't make the switch off the Jacksonville bus at Ocala. The clerk at the bus terminal here tracked it down — it's sitting in Fort Lauderdale!"

I was a lot less upset than I had been two days earlier. "Oh, well. Between all the Sleepover Friends, I've got plenty of stuff to wear," I said.

"Are you feeling okay, Stephanie?" Kate asked.

Finally we turned onto Ocean Street and up our drive. It had been a long day, and I was dying to get the Sleepover Friends together and discuss the Josh problem. Maybe right after dinner we could put our heads together.

When we got to the house, Uncle Nick left the van's headlights on so we wouldn't fall going up the steps. On the screened porch, Tara took her keys out of her shoulder bag, reached for the door, and stopped. "Uh-oh. Nick, here we go again. It's not locked." Tara pushed the door, and it swung open with a creak, into the still, dark house.

"Are you sure you locked it?" Uncle Nick said. "We were all pretty sleepy when we left this morning."

"I'm certain," Tara said a little nervously.

"Girls, get back in the van," Uncle Nick said. We weren't about to argue. We ran down the stairs and locked ourselves in the van.

"What is it *now*?" Lauren moaned. "It's starting to get dark out, and here we are, trapped in the middle of nowhere with no phone — and who knows what's still lurking in the house? What if something happens to Uncle Nick and Tara? What if someone's *still* in there?" She started biting her fingernails, staring through the dusk at the house.

"Oh, Lauren, hush up!" Kate snapped. "We're all worried, but you don't have to make it worse."

Personally, I thought Lauren was just saying out loud what we were all thinking privately, but it *was* pretty creepy. All we could do was wait, though.

Once we were safely in the van, we saw Uncle Nick reach around the front door frame to flip on the living room light switch. But nothing happened. "The lights aren't working," we heard him say grimly.

"We've got a big flashlight under the front seat." Tara ran down the steps and we let her into the van.

She reached in and dug out the huge, eight-battery flashlight.

Back on the porch, she handed it to Uncle Nick, and he shone it through the door into the living room. Then Uncle Nick said something we couldn't hear. Tara nodded and hitched her purse up higher on her shoulder. Then she turned around and said, "Girls, you stay there for a minute, okay?" We all nodded.

Uncle Nick pushed open the door the rest of the way, and they both disappeared inside.

"Why did *both* of them have to . . ." Lauren began, but Kate turned around and stared at her, and Lauren trailed off.

"I'm sure they know what they're doing, you guys," Patti said softly. "Everything's going to be fine."

Maybe so, but I didn't *breathe* until I saw Uncle Nick and Tara pop back out onto the porch again.

"All clear," they called to us.

In a second we had jumped out of the car and were dashing up the steps. The four of us crowded around the open door and peered inside, following the beam of Uncle Nick's flashlight.

"Wow!" Kate gasped. The four of us barely breathed. The living room had been totally wrecked!

Chapter 13

Our eyes followed the beam of the light as it moved across the living room. The wrought-iron coffee table was lying on its side, the glass top shattered. Cushions from the old couch were tossed around the room. And the point of Aunt Mary's machete was buried in one of the couch's wooden arms. The flashlight beam glittered on the machete's sharp, shiny edge, and a chill ran down my spine.

Even though it was a warm night, Lauren's teeth were chattering. "The g-ghost!" she managed to choke out. "It doesn't want us staying here!"

"Lauren, be realistic!" Kate said. "Obviously, the burglars came back. Don't you think, Tara?" Kate was speaking bravely, but even in the dim light I could see that her eyes were wide and round. I'm sure I looked the same way. I couldn't believe that people had come and destroyed everything like this.

126

What if they were still around? What if they were hiding in the woods right in the back of the house?

"There really wasn't much left for burglars to take," Tara said slowly.

"Hold on, you guys. You wait here, and let me go check the fuse box. I'll be right back," Uncle Nick said, stepping forward into the blackness. I could hear his footsteps as he slowly made his way toward the back of the house. All the hairs on the back of my neck were standing up. I reached out and touched Patti's arm, and she patted my hand.

The five of us huddled on the screened porch.

"How're you doing, girls?" Tara asked in a shaky voice.

"We're okay," Patti said weakly.

"We're fine," Kate added. *Speak for yourself,* I thought.

Suddenly, practically every light in the house flashed on! Uncle Nick had fixed the fuse box. The five of us walked through the door into the living room.

"What a mess!" Kate whispered.

She wasn't kidding. The place looked like a tornado had hit it! Pots and pans from the kitchen had been flung around the living room. So had most of the groceries we'd bought. I had never seen such a mess in all my life.

Uncle Nick came back. "Somebody — "

"Or something!" Lauren murmured.

"Flipped the switch in the fuse box to turn off all the lights," Uncle Nick reported. "And ripped the phone out of the wall in the bedroom — not that it was working, anyway. Tara, don't you think we should drive straight back to town? We could book some rooms in Grandy's Grand Hotel. And we could report the whole thing to Sheriff Gunn right away."

"The sheriff should definitely be told as soon as possible. But there's no way anybody's going to force me out of my own house, Nick," Tara said, quavery but determined.

"That goes for me, too, Uncle Nick," Patti said, which was a lot braver than I was feeling.

"What do you think went on here?" Tara asked. "Maybe the burglars did come back, to see what else they could take. Then something startled them — maybe when Greg Grandy stopped by — and they left in a big hurry."

"I don't know," Uncle Nick said slowly. "This doesn't seem like ordinary, run-of-the-mill burglars. I mean, why would they have stuck the machete into the couch?" He shook his head.

"It's as though someone is trying to scare us off," Tara said quietly.

As far as I was concerned, they were doing an excellent job!

"Let's look at the bedrooms," Uncle Nick said.

The bedrooms were smaller, and there'd been less to mess up. But all our suitcases (except mine, which was spending a quiet night in Fort Lauderdale) had been opened, and the clothes thrown all over the place. Plus, my sleeping bag had been ripped from top to bottom, and so had Patti's. The stuffing was all over the place.

"Oh, dear," Tara said, surveying the wreckage. "You guys, I'm so sorry about all this. . . . Patti, you and Stephanie can't manage without your sleeping bags. Maybe we had better go back to town after all, and . . ."

If Patti could be brave, I could, too. "It's not your fault, Tara," I said. "Patti and I can push two beds together, zip together what's left of our sleeping bags, and share it as a quilt."

"And the clothes are fine," Kate said, flipping her suitcase over. "Just a little wrinkled . . . YEOOOOW!" She suddenly dropped the suitcase like a hot coal and screamed, "SSSSSSNAKES!"

Out of the corner of my eye, I saw what looked like a red, black, and yellow garden hose slowly uncoiling on the floor. In half a second, I was out of the bedroom, out of the living room, out of the house, and up on the hood of the van!

Kate was right behind me. "I practically t-t-touched it!" she yelled, shuddering. "I could be d-dead!" She grabbed onto my shoulder for support.

129

"Kate, it didn't bite you, did it?" Tara had run out after us, so pale that even her lips looked white.

Lauren ran up, wailing, "Patti's still in there. Patti? Patti!"

"Here I am." Patti hurried down the front steps. "At first I thought it might be a coral snake, and coral snakes are poisonous. But the colored bands are arranged in the wrong order: 'Red and yellow kill a fellow, red and black venom lack.' "

"Do you hear that? You're all right, Kate!" Tara said reassuringly, giving her a hug. Kate took a deep breath and nodded, and Tara helped her into the front seat of the van.

"Everybody in," Tara said to the rest of us.

"Where are we going?" I asked, practically vaulting into the back.

"Grandy's Grand," Uncle Nick said. "Even though the snake was nonpoisonous, the message was clear. Somebody wants us to leave."

"And we're going to let them?" Kate said, feeling a lot stronger now that she knew she wasn't going to be sharing her room with a snake. Well, at least not a *poisonous* snake.

"Just for tonight, we'll sleep at the hotel," Uncle Nick told us. "But first, I'm coming back here to rig up a quick and easy burglar alarm." As I mentioned, Uncle Nick is a terrific inventor. "Any uninvited visitors will get a very nasty shock, indeed!"

Tara and Uncle Nick wouldn't let us go back into the house that night for supplies, in case there were any other nasty surprises planned for us. So we drove away with just the bare necessities that she'd collected for us: toothbrushes, toothpaste, some odd combinations of outfits from the clothes dumped on the floor, and five clean, snake-less T-shirts of Uncle Nick's that she'd grabbed for us to sleep in.

The room we ended up with at Grandy's Grand only had two full-size beds in it. Tara and Uncle Nick were going to take one, Patti and I were taking the other, and Lauren and Kate would be on the floor, since they still had their sleeping bags — carefully shaken out and examined!

When we got up to our room, Patti, Lauren, Kate, and I absolutely collapsed on one bed. I don't think I'd ever been so tired in all my life. My emotions felt as if they had gone through a bigger roller coaster than the one at Wonderworld! We had gotten up really early that morning, spent the whole day at Wonderworld suspecting Josh of horrible crimes, and finally faced the mess at Aunt Mary's house, finishing off with reptiles in the luggage. I had been scared, happy, nervous, excited, and then terrified, all in one day. If I wanted to be an actress, this was great training.

Uncle Nick and Tara had gone downstairs to try to get some dinner for us, and report the house-wrecking to Sheriff Gunn. I finally had a chance to tell Kate and Patti about Josh's mom.

"Listen, you guys," I said wearily.

"It had to be the burglars," Kate mumbled. She was lying across the end of the bed, face up, her eyes closed.

"Listen, about Josh — " I tried again.

"But what Tara said was true. There was nothing valuable left for the burglars to take," Patti pointed out, ignoring me. She was lying on her stomach next to Kate, her chin on her fists. "And they would have known that."

"No, not to take anything," Lauren said sleepily. "The guy from the store in Hoopin' Holler called his 'suppliers,' and they decided to give us a warning."

"But what's weird is that it had to be different people from the first burglars," Kate said, propping herself up a little.

"Why's that?" I asked. If we weren't going to talk about Josh, we might as well get to the bottom of this burglar thing.

"Because," Kate said, her narrowed eyes gleaming, "our phone wires had already been cut on the outside, days ago. Whoever was in the house tonight pulled the phone from the wall. They *didn't know* that the wires had been cut!" She sat back and looked at us all expectantly.

"Am I supposed to feel better that there are *two*

sets of burglars?" I demanded. "Anyway, that sounds like a gangster movie to me, Kate." I was lying on my stomach, too, my head hanging over the edge of the bed.

"Was that snake real, or not?" Kate said huffily.

"Oh, it was real, all right," I said. "I think somebody is definitely trying to scare us. But I don't think it's burglars at all."

Lauren raised her head off a mound of pillows. "Aunt Mary's ghost?" she said, surprised that someone was agreeing with her at last.

"No, not Aunt Mary's ghost," I snorted. "Greg Grandy."

"Greg Grandy!" That woke everybody up!

"Get real, Stephanie!" said Kate. Kate's usually our detective, so she was probably a little miffed that she hadn't thought of it herself.

"Why Greg Grandy?" Patti asked.

"Think about it," I said. "Tara has something he wants: Aunt Mary's property."

"Yes," Patti said, with me so far.

"She says she won't sell, so he harps on a neighborhood ghost to make her change her mind," I said. "He probably started those rumors himself!"

"What about the lady in the grocery store? She mentioned weird noises and strange lights," Lauren argued.

"Both of which could have been caused by the

original burglars," I said. "If someone heard those noises just once, it would be enough to start rumors."

"Hmmm," Patti said. "You may be right."

"Who else could it be? We know it wasn't the Marcuses. They were at Wonderworld all day today. They couldn't have done it."

"The Marcuses?" Kate sat up. "What on earth are you talking about?"

Lauren and I told Patti and Kate all about Mrs. Marcus's weird telephone conversation. I reminded them how excited she was to find out we had a manatee in our creek. And how they had changed their vacation plans just to come over to Puerto Delfin and take a look.

"All the same," I concluded, "we know they weren't here today. But maybe they're in league with Mr. Grandy. . . ." My mind wandered down this interesting path for a minute. "Mr. Grandy's probably the one who convinced the mayor that Tara's property would be too expensive for the town to take care of as a wildlife preserve," I said. "Now he thinks he'll scare us good, and we'll head back to the frozen north. He doesn't know that *we* know about the manatees. . . ."

"Maybe," Patti said. "He does seem to be hanging around a lot."

"That's true," said Lauren. "Didn't he mention

that he'd stopped by the house today while we were out? He had plenty of time to wreck the place."

"And then admit to us that he was there? That doesn't make sense," Kate argued.

"Of course it does," I said. "He figured we'd all think what you're thinking — that he'd never admit he had stopped by if he were really guilty."

Just then, Tara and Uncle Nick came back with our dinner: ham and cheese sandwiches, apples, and a bottle of fruit juice. They nodded seriously when we told them about our suspicions.

"You know, I think I agree with you," Tara said.

"Grandy's certainly first on my list," Uncle Nick said. "But there's a problem with that. I found a big, muddy footprint in the kitchen, in front of the closet with the fuse box."

"A muddy footprint definitely eliminates your ghost, Lauren," Kate said.

"Couldn't that be Mr. Grandy's footprint?" I said.

"Not unless he has a large accomplice," Tara said. "You know how short he is. He probably has small feet. Uncle Nick said the footprint was larger than his own foot."

"And I don't have dainty feet, not by any means," Uncle Nick said, grinning.

So if it wasn't a ghost — and if it wasn't Greg

Grandy — who was it? We were back to the burglars, whoever they were!

After what we had been through, I think we all fell asleep about two seconds after our heads hit our pillows. After dinner, Uncle Nick had gone back to the house to rig up a burglar alarm, but I didn't even hear him sneak back into our room. When I got up the next morning, I found out that he and Tara had already seen the sheriff.

It turned out that Sheriff Gunn had some news. "The Hoopin' Holler sheriff checked out the owner of the antique store," Uncle Nick told us. "It seems he's honest, and so is his supplier. The supplier had no idea where the table came from originally. He picked it up a couple of months ago at an auction in northern Florida near Jacksonville."

Uncle Nick glanced around the hotel room at the four of us. "Sheriff Gunn also suggests that we keep this hotel room for the rest of our vacation, or at least until we know who is behind the mess at our house. We can go shopping, explore the town, visit the lighthouse. . . ."

"What about your burglar alarm, Uncle Nick?" Kate interrupted him. "Is it working?"

"Like a charm," Uncle Nick said with a modest grin. "A cricket couldn't get into that house without making a huge racket."

"That's good enough for me," Kate said bravely.

"Us, too," Patti, Lauren, and I said together. I felt a tiny bit better in the daylight.

"We have the manatees to keep an eye on," I said.

"And the reef to explore," said Patti.

"You're sure?" Tara asked, looking relieved.

"Certain," we replied.

So Tara checked us out of the hotel. We stopped at the diner and had some breakfast, then headed back to Aunt Mary's house.

Chapter
14

From the outside, the house looked just the same. It was hard to believe that it was so messed up inside.

"You're sure there are no more snakes?" Kate asked as we lingered a little nervously outside the front door.

"Not with this burglar alarm." Uncle Nick pointed down at his feet, where two thin silver wires ran across the screened porch from one end to the other. One lay directly on the wooden floor, the other was suspended at a little less than knee height.

"I took our slithery guest out to the canal. And none crawled in after that, or I would have known about it. These wires completely circle the house."

"How do they work?" Patti asked.

"Touch one, and you'll see," her uncle said with a grin.

"And HEAR!" Tara shouted over the clanging that began as soon as Patti's leg brushed the top wire. And all the lights in the house were flashing on and off, as if it were a giant pinball machine!

From his back pocket, Uncle Nick pulled out a remote control, like the ones used for television sets, and switched off the alarm. He looked very pleased with himself.

"How did you manage to throw this together last night with no equipment?" Tara said to her husband, amazed, once the clanging had died down.

"Sheriff Gunn lent me a car alarm," Uncle Nick said. "The wire was already in the house — I'd used some on the hot water heater — and I found the remote in our bedroom. There probably used to be a TV in this house, too, before our burglars came along."

"Well, your alarm system will certainly keep anybody else from poking around," Tara said.

My ears were still ringing as we stepped carefully over the wires and into the living room.

"Well, let's get to it," Kate said briskly, rolling up her sleeves. I met Lauren's and Patti's eyes, and we all smirked. This was probably Kate's favorite part of the whole vacation. Tara collected mops and brooms and buckets, and we all started cleaning up and putting things away.

Uncle Nick swept up the broken glass from the

coffee table and replaced it with a couple of boards. I put the cushions back on the old couch, and Tara put Aunt Mary's machete back where it belonged. Just looking at that blade was a creepy reminder.

Patti picked up all of the pots and pans that had been thrown around the living room, and Kate mopped up the mess of flour, milk, and coffee and whatever else had been dumped on the floor. Then we folded up Kate's, Patti's, and Lauren's clothes and put them on the beds in our bedrooms.

That's when I remembered the muddy footprint. "Uncle Nick, is the footprint gone, the one outside the closet door in the kitchen?" I asked him.

"No, I had saved it for the sheriff to see, and I haven't gotten around to mopping it up yet," Uncle Nick said. "Want to take a look at it?"

The four of us and Tara crowded into the kitchen. "Well, whoever it was, he certainly has enormous feet," Tara said. The print looked as long as both of my feet put together!

"It was the Swamp Thing!" Lauren said, and we managed to laugh a little.

"I think it was made by someone wearing rubber boots," Uncle Nick said. "See the ridges in the bottom? And how round the toe is? It definitely looks like a rubber boot to me. The guy's real feet might be a bit smaller. Now, where did I leave the mop and pail?"

Uncle Nick headed for the living room with Tara, but Kate, Lauren, Patti, and I kneeled down to take a closer look at the print.

"So this is the jerk who stuck a snake in my suitcase," Kate said angrily.

"I still think it could be Greg Grandy," I said. "Maybe he put on big rubber boots over his little feet, just to throw us off the trail."

"I guess it's definitely not a ghost causing the trouble," Lauren said, disappointed. She reached out to touch the very real dried mud caked near the toe of the print.

"Wait — " Patti pulled Lauren's hand back and carefully picked a piece of green stuff out of the mud. "This is beach grass. And look at the heel — there's a little V-shaped notch cut out of it."

"One side, ladies." Uncle Nick was back with the bucket full of soapy water and the mop. We stood up, and he splashed some of the water out of the pail onto the footprint. "This is the last we'll ever see of our burglar in Aunt Mary's house," he said. "I stand behind every one of Uncle Nick's Super Alarm Systems ever made!"

We cleaned for a while, then the four of us drove back into town with Tara. She dropped us off at Beauty and the Beach to browse, while she went on to Haines's Grocery to get lunch supplies for the Marcuses.

"You guys, should we tell Tara and Uncle Nick about Mrs. Marcus?" I asked the others as we waited for Tara in front of the store.

"Well," Patti said, "Uncle Nick usually has good instincts about people. He seems to think the Marcuses are okay."

"Just to be sure, though, I think we should stick to them like glue," Kate said firmly. "And if we can't stay by *them*, we should take turns watching the creek — so we'll be sure to see anyone who tries to take Tug."

"In the meantime, let's act natural," Patti said.

Lauren and I saluted. "Aye, aye, ma'am!" We all laughed.

When Tara pulled up in front of our house, we saw that the Marcuses were already there. I sighed. "Let's go, guys."

I have to admit — both Josh and his brother Troy looked great.

"Girls, why don't you take Josh and Troy exploring while we get lunch together?" Tara suggested.

"Yeah, let's go look at the creek. Maybe we could try to catch a glimpse of Tug and his mother," Josh said.

I looked at Kate, Patti, and Lauren, and Patti shrugged as if to say, *What can we do?*

So we started making our way down the little path. Josh went crazy about how much the place looked like a real jungle, the wild noises the birds and animals made, and how natural it all seemed. "It's fantastic that we're only a couple of miles from downtown Puerto Delfin," he exclaimed. "In here it's like being in a rain forest in South America. What a great park this'll make." *He seems so sincere,* I thought.

As luck would have it, Tug and his mom *did* show up while we were at the creek. We were crouching down on the bank of the creek where Lauren and I had first seen Tug — carefully hidden behind some bushes — waiting for what seemed like forever. Troy grumbled first about his bug bites — "By the time I get home, I'm going to look like I have terminal acne!" — and the creek — "What is all this green muck? It stinks. . . . It's like camping on a dump!" — and the heat — "I can't believe I could be skiing right now, at Michelle's house in Vermont!"

Josh rolled his eyes at me, and I could see Kate getting more and more annoyed. She was just about to tell Troy off when we heard a deep sigh from down the creek.

"I think Tug's coming!" Lauren whispered. We all held our breaths.

There was another loud sigh, and the splash of a thick flipper. Suddenly a broad greenish-gray back

143

heaved slowly into view. A *very* broad back — it was Tug's mom!

"There she is!" Patti whispered. I was awe-struck. She was so big, yet so graceful as she glided through the water. Then I remembered that this beautiful creature could be in danger — from the very people we were showing her to!

"Wow," I heard Troy whisper as a second greenish-gray back curved out of the water for a second and vanished. Then a small, familiar, round head appeared. He was bald, with two sad brown eyes, a snub nose, and bristly whiskers.

"Tug," Kate whispered.

"He's great!" Josh whispered back.

The mother manatee popped up at Tug's side. They gazed at each other for a few seconds. Then the two of them actually hugged each other with their flippers.

"Ooh!" Patti and Lauren exclaimed softly.

But it was just loud enough for the manatees to hear. They took a last deep breath and sank into the creek.

"Show's over," said Troy. "Pretty cool." He stood up, dusted off his pants, and slouched back up the creek toward the house.

"Sorry for scaring them off," Lauren and Patti apologized sheepishly to the rest of us.

I couldn't blame them. Those manatees hugging

each other was one of the sweetest things I'd ever seen.

Josh moved closer to the creek to take one last look, then bent down to pull at something hooked to a tree root growing into the water.

"What's that?" Kate asked.

"Looks like a piece of fishnet," Josh said, pulling up three or four feet of black netting and letting it drop back into the creek with a splash. "It's torn."

"I'll bet it's been here for years," Patti said. "Before Aunt Mary's time. The creek narrows at this point." The far bank was only about fifteen or twenty feet away from us. "Fishermen probably strung nets across to trap the fish that swam into the canal at high tide."

We headed back to the house for lunch. Then we lounged around in the shade for a while, letting everything digest while the Marcuses assembled their scuba equipment for an afternoon on the reef. It was strange, but Mrs. Marcus didn't seem that interested in looking at Tug herself.

Finally we were all ready to head to the beach. On top of masks, fins, and snorkels like the ones we used for snorkeling, the Marcuses had bulky, life jacket-type things called buoyancy control devices. Not to mention scuba tanks that weighed about fifty pounds each, tank valves, backpacks, regulators, weight belts — I could go on and on! Add a couple of underwater cameras, and it was like going on a safari just to get everything from Aunt Mary's house to the beach.

This time we didn't follow the creek, but stuck to the trail since it's a straighter route. Uncle Nick took the lead with the machete, and Tara the rear, in case anybody got caught on a palm frond. Everyone was so loaded down with gear that there was a lot of stumbling and staggering.

But we finally made it to the Gulf, and we actually had an excellent afternoon, all things considering. Not even the Goodwins in their old camper showed up; Uncle Nick made a joke about them being too busy bathing in their two tubs.

I forgot to worry about looking like a geek in my snorkeling gear. After all, the Marcuses were wearing more weird stuff than I was! Mr. and Mrs. Marcus snapped lots of photos of us underwater on the reef — which would be great to show the kids back home in cold, wintery Riverhurst. Above water, Kate took about a zillion feet of videotape, including lots of beach scenes of Josh and Troy. Troy and Kate actually discovered that they had a lot of the same movie likes and dislikes.

At sunset we went back to the house and arranged to meet the Marcuses at the Beachtree Inn on Front Street for dinner. I borrowed a pair of overalls from Lauren, and a yellow T-shirt of Kate's. Looking at myself in the mirror, I could hardly believe that only a week ago I would rather have *died* than wear something that wasn't red, black, or white.

"Say guys, what do you think of the Marcuses?" I asked.

Patti frowned. "I don't know. They didn't seem to want to find Tug. . . . " she said.

"I noticed that, too," I said. "But they sure did know a lot about all the things down by the reef. Mrs. Marcus sounded like a walking textbook."

"I guess she'd *have* to know all that stuff if she's been kidnapping sea mammals all over the place," Lauren said suspiciously. I shrugged my shoulders and tied a sweatshirt around my waist.

Dinner was really good — I ate so many shrimp I thought I was going to explode. The Marcuses made plans to explore the reef again the next day, then Mrs. Marcus said, "And maybe we could walk along the creek and try to catch a glimpse of your wild manatees. It would be interesting to see if they're as big and healthy as the ones in Wonderworld."

I sat bolt upright. Maybe Mrs. Marcus was going to make her move tomorrow. Patti caught my eye and nodded slightly. I knew we'd have to get together later and make our plans.

As we were walking back out to our cars, Tara

said, "I know what! Josh, why don't you and Troy camp out in our yard tonight, so you'll be on the spot for the beach tomorrow?"

"Wow! That sounds great. Mom, can we?" Josh asked.

"I think I'll pass," Troy said. "I've had enough of the outdoors for one day."

So it was settled. Josh got his things out of the Marcuses' car and rode back to Aunt Mary's house with us. Uncle Nick helped him set up his tent, and Tara gave him a flashlight. Then Uncle Nick showed Josh how to avoid setting off the alarms, in case he needed anything during the night.

"Okay, thanks, Mr. Pollard," Josh said.

"Good-night," we all said.

Chapter
15

It seemed to take ages for everyone to brush their teeth and get ready for bed. Then we all told Uncle Nick and Tara good-night, and headed for our bedrooms. We turned off our lights and waited about fifteen minutes, then Kate and Lauren quietly creaked open their door and snuck over to Patti's and my room.

We sat on my bed in the dark, discussing what we should do.

"Why don't we split up into two groups, and go keep watch by the creek?" Kate suggested.

"No," Lauren said firmly. "Number one, the Marcuses probably won't do anything until tomorrow anyway. Number two, there is *no* way that I'm going to go creeping around in that jungle in the dark."

"Now, Lauren," Kate started to argue.

"No, Kate. I think Lauren's right," Patti said. "I

know Uncle Nick wouldn't want us to go to the creek at night by ourselves. There really isn't that much we can do."

We never really did settle anything, and finally Kate and Lauren went back to their room, and Patti and I settled down to sleep. It was hard for me to stop thinking about Tug and his mom, but I must have drifted off. Then, all of a sudden, CLANG CLANG CLANG!!! The alarm was going off!!

Patti and I jumped up in a flash. All the lights in the house were blinking on and off, and those awful car sirens were wailing! We dashed out into the hall in time to see Uncle Nick and Tara pulling on their robes as they raced to the living room. He had his remote, and he clicked it once. The awful sirens died down.

"What is it?" I yelled.

Lauren and Kate were right behind us. "What's going on?" Lauren asked, rubbing her eyes.

"I don't know," I said.

Uncle Nick ran to the front door and pulled it open. There, standing in the light of the screen porch, was —

"Josh!" Uncle Nick cried. "Are you all right? Did you set off the alarm?"

Josh quickly stepped into the living room. He had his sleeping bag wrapped around him, and he looked pretty scared.

"Yeah, I did — sorry. I set it off on purpose, to scare that guy away."

"What guy?" cried Tara, pulling Josh to the couch and making him sit down. Uncle Nick shut and locked the front door.

"Well, I was out there asleep, when I think a noise woke me up. It sounded like an engine of some kind, and it was getting closer. I poked my head out of the tent to see what was going on." Josh paused and hunched his shoulders up with the memory. "I looked into the woods, and there was some weird, greenish-yellow light bobbing through the trees."

"The green light again!" Patti whispered in my ear.

"Do you think it could have been swamp gas?" I asked Josh hopefully.

He frowned and said, "But I heard a motor, too. Then I heard something, or someone, start to crash through the trees — coming in this direction!" Josh stopped a moment and kind of shivered. Tara reached out and patted his arm.

"It seemed to be coming closer, and I could see the light clearly. I could almost make out the figure of at least one person. . . ." He stopped and looked sheepish. "Then I guess I panicked, because I ran up on the porch and grabbed the alarm wire, to set it off."

"You did the right thing," Uncle Nick assured

him. He went and opened the front door again, peering out into the night. "There doesn't seem to be anything out there now," he said. "I guess the alarm worked." Josh smiled weakly, and Kate, Patti, Lauren, and I looked at each other with round eyes.

"Well, that was an awful scare you had," Tara said briskly, getting up. "But you're safe now, because we're all here. Let's just settle you down here on the couch, then tomorrow morning we'll go look for evidence of the intruder in the woods."

Uncle Nick nodded grimly. "This has gone far enough!" he growled. "Tomorrow we're getting to the bottom of this whole thing, and that's that!" I wouldn't like to be the intruder and have to face Uncle Nick looking like that!

We got Josh settled, then went back to our rooms and tried to go back to sleep. I felt better knowing that Uncle Nick's alarm worked as well as it did. I didn't know who was sneaking around out there in the dark, but at least I knew that Josh wasn't in on it.

The next time I opened my eyes, it was barely light outside. I looked around sleepily to see what had woken me up, and saw that Patti was already dressed and pulling on her sneakers. "What are you doing?" I said drowsily.

"I just realized something about an important

152

clue, over by the creek," Patti replied. "Go back to sleep."

Sure, like I was going to let her wander around in the jungle by herself. I climbed out of bed and pulled on the clothes I'd worn the night before. Then I splashed cold water on my face to wake myself up. When I crept past the other bedroom, I could hear Lauren and Kate snoring in their sleeping bags. Then I stumbled down the hall toward the back door.

"Not that way," Patti whispered, turning me around. "We'll set off the alarm again."

"Can't we get Uncle Nick, or at least Josh? Or even Kate and Lauren?" I asked softly.

"There isn't time — if I'm right, Tug is already in big trouble," Patti said. We ended up pushing our bedroom window all the way up and jumping out over the wires. Then we padded over the dewy grass toward the creek path.

The jungle was really noisy at daybreak. All the birds were chirping and squawking and making a racket, greeting the sun. We made our way through the jungle. At least most of the brush had been cleared away. I kept looking all around to make sure nothing was sneaking up on us. My heart was beating up in my throat, and cold, nervous sweat had broken out on my forehead. Every time Patti stepped on a twig, I jumped about a foot in the air. With each step, I felt more afraid. I was really, really, sorry we hadn't woken anybody else up.

But it was too late. If I went back for help, Patti would be left alone — there was no way she'd turn back now. Finally we reached the bank of the creek. Patti started walking toward the ocean. Then we heard the manatee — great, loud sighing breaths.

"Listen to that," Patti said. "Tug sounds excited about something!"

We crouched down as low as we could and hurried along in kind of a running walk to where we usually saw him. When we straightened up a little to peek over a fern, though, we saw that it wasn't Tug who was making those sounds. It was the adult manatee, his mom. She looked frantic!

First she scanned both banks of the creek, as if she were looking for something. Then she took a deep breath and did a jackknife straight down into the murky water, her big round tail slapping the surface like a giant beaver's. A minute later, she popped back up, took another deep breath, and peered anxiously at the creek banks again. We watched her for several minutes, and Tug didn't surface at all, not once!

"Where is Tug?" Patti said exactly what I was thinking.

"Napping?" I said hopefully, although I didn't really believe it.

"With his mom zooming back and forth? I don't think so," Patti said worriedly.

We stood up a little farther, and Tug's mom spotted us. She disappeared with hardly a ripple.

That's when I noticed the end of a fishnet lying on the creek bank. "Josh dropped that net back into the water, didn't he?" I said.

"Right! And that's the clue I suddenly remembered," Patti said. The two of us scrambled out of the greenery. "He dropped a net into the water all right," Patti said, picking up the piece of netting. "But look. Stephanie, if this net were old, wouldn't it be covered with seaweed and algae, like everything else in the creek?" My eyes grew wide as I saw where her thoughts were leading us.

"Plus, it would be pretty rotten by now, after years of soaking in water. And it's not. It looks brand-new!" I said. The black cord that the net was made of was strong and shiny. "Patti — do you think the green light at night is somebody fishing by stringing a fishnet across the creek, the way they did in the old days?"

"Fish are attracted to light," Patti nodded. "They would swim toward it, and get stuck in the net, and all the fishermen would have to do is . . . oh, no!" she exclaimed. "Tug could get stuck in the net, too, and drown! Manatees have to breathe every few minutes. What if he's hung up down there right now?!"

The two of us grabbed the wet net and started hauling. But after we'd pulled in six or seven feet of it, it ended as cleanly as if it had been snipped off with a pair of scissors.

We both collapsed on the creek bank. "Whew! That thing is heavy!" I puffed. "But at least we know Tug's not caught in the net." The sun was coming up, and the air was already starting to get heavy and warm.

"Wait! Look, footprints." Patti was gazing down at the damp clay where we were sitting. "Rubber boot footprints!" Sure enough, there were footprints all around us, with ridges and round toes.

"Patti, there's even a notch cut out of the heel! This fisherman is the same guy who wrecked our house!" I said. "But why?"

Patti was following the footprints on her hands and knees. "He wasn't alone — there are some smaller prints next to the big ones," she said. "They're heading down the creek bank toward the beach! Beach grass was stuck in the footprint in our kitchen, remember?"

"I'll bet these guys are the ones who started the ghost stories to keep people away. They come here at night and string their nets across Aunt Mary's creek. Then they turn on their light, and catch the fish that swim in to look at the light," I began.

"Pull in their nets full of fish, carry them to the beach, load them into a truck, and drive safely away," Patti finished grimly. "First of all, they have no business being on this property — it's private. Secondly, nets are really dangerous for the manatees." Patti sounded angrier than I'd ever heard her! "And dolphins. Maybe that's why Aunt Mary's dolphins have disappeared! And where is Tug?"

She stood up and stalked down the creek toward the beach.

"Hang on!" I was trotting to catch up with her. I tried one more time: "Shouldn't we be telling Uncle Nick and Tara about this?"

"I want to check out the beach first. These people could still be hanging around!" Patti said sternly.

That seemed like an even better reason for us to get help. But there was no stopping Patti. "They could disappear, and we'd never know who they were!" she said, which I had to agree with.

"Okay, but let's be cool about it," I cautioned. "Let's sneak up to the beach, not burst right out of the trees on top of them!" Patti slowed down, and we made our way more cautiously along the trail.

When we got to the edge of the sand, I peeked through the bushes and saw the Goodwin's rusty old camper. "It's just the Goodwins," I said.

Luckily, Patti pulled me back just in time. "Stephanie, these fishermen we're looking for just might *be* the Goodwins!" she whispered. "Remember those two big bathtubs they bought? They could be keeping the fish alive in the tubs until they can sell them!"

"Wow!" I murmured. "Close call! But why would they still be sitting here, risking getting caught?"

We had the answer to that pretty quickly. The Goodwins were having engine trouble with their rusty old bucket-of-bolts! Mr. Goodwin was bending over with his head under the hood of the camper. Mrs. Goodwin was inside the cab, in the driver's seat, turning the ignition. The motor was coughing and sputtering.

"Now what?" I said to Patti.

"If they get it started, they'll leave, and we might never know what they were up to at that creek!" Patti said. "I'm going to take a look into the camper through the back door."

"What if they see you?" I exclaimed. I was remembering how Mrs. Goodwin had acted when she caught Kate and me peeking in at their bathtubs — plenty nasty! No wonder she'd freaked out — she had a guilty conscience!

"I'm hoping they'll be too busy to notice me," Patti said. Patti may be quiet and shy, but she's very determined when she sets her mind to something.

"Then I'm coming with you," I said, squaring

my shoulders. If the Goodwins did notice us, they were going to have *two* Sleepover Friends to deal with!

We crept across the sand, careful to keep the camper between us and them. Patti put her finger to her lips and pointed down to the ground: rubber boot prints led us straight to the back of the camper. She climbed up on the back step, cupped her hands around her eyes, and stared inside through the dusty glass.

"Hurry!" I whispered as the motor coughed and almost caught. "Do you see anything?"

"There's definitely something in one of the tubs," she whispered. "It's filled to the brim with water, and . . . Tug!!!"

"Whaaaat?!" I squeezed onto the step beside her and peered in, too.

"They've got Tug in there!" Patti murmured, her voice shaking. "He just raised his little head for a breath."

"I see him, I see him!" I whispered, horrified. The baby manatee was lying on his back, practically filling the whole tub farthest from the door. His mournful brown eyes were just above the waterline. No wonder his mother was so frantic — the Goodwins had kidnapped her baby! "Patti, what are we going to do?!"

I thought quickly. Maybe Patti should hide in

the bushes and keep an eye on the Goodwins while I ran back to the house for help. No, maybe *I* should stay at the beach, and *Patti* could run back for help, since she runs twice as fast as I do. Or should we *both* go for help, and hope the Goodwins couldn't start the van? Or . . .

But the answer was decided for us. Before we had a chance to make up our minds, a voice yelled from up the beach, "Hey! Good morning! Have you seen two girls around here? One has dark, curly hair, and the other one's taller, with light brown hair." It was Josh Marcus, calling out to the Goodwins — which meant everyone at the house had missed us and had sent him after us. It made me feel a little braver. But now the Goodwins had been warned that we might be wandering around, and they'd be on the lookout for us.

"Should we yell to Josh?" Patti whispered. Two angry adults against three trespassing kids? Definitely not a good idea.

"No! If we show ourselves, all three of us could be in major hot water!" I whispered to Patti. Back to the bushes? The Goodwins would surely see us. "Quick — inside!"

I pulled open the back door to the camper, and we practically fell into the empty bathtub, our sneakers thumping on the floor. I held my breath. Had the Goodwins heard us?

Suddenly, the camper's motor stopped coughing and hacking for a second. We froze with the door hanging open. We couldn't move a hair.

Mr. Goodwin had ignored Josh's question about us. But Mrs. Goodwin was saying, "No, we haven't seen anybody on the beach, except the sea gulls."

We held our breaths, waiting for Josh to reply. "If you bump into them, please tell them we're waiting for them for breakfast, okay?"

Breakfast! I imagined Kate and Lauren, just crawling out of their cozy sleeping bags, safe and sound with Uncle Nick and Tara. . . . So near, and yet so far. And here *we* were, tracking down criminals who were stealing an endangered animal! Just then, the Goodwin's engine coughed again . . . and caught.

Beatrice must have stepped on the gas pedal, because the engine suddenly roared. "We can't help you — we're leaving," she said briskly.

Patti and I rolled our eyes at each other. "We'll have to jump out before they really get moving," she whispered in my ear. "The sand will be soft." The sand will be soft? As compared to what? Since when was Patti so casual about leaping out of a moving vehicle? I gulped.

"Thanks, anyway," Josh said, his voice growing fainter as he turned away.

"Let's get out of here," Mr. Goodwin rumbled.

"He's coming this way," I whispered to Patti.

"Close the door — we'll scoot under the bed," Patti hissed.

The back door of the van squeaked a little as I pushed it partway closed. My heart was banging like a drum! I thought there was no way I was going to fit under that bunk. But somehow Patti and I both squeezed in between the side of the empty tub and one of the beds. Then we wedged ourselves beneath the bedframe. The next thing we heard was the back door slamming shut!

Another door slammed up front, and the old camper started to bump slowly across the sand. "Quick! Now's our chance to get out of here!" Patti barely breathed the words in my ear.

We scrambled out from under the bunk and stared down at poor Tug for a second. "We'll save you, Tug," we whispered to the pitiful-looking baby manatee.

Now all we had to do was pretend we were professional stuntwomen and bail out of a moving camper — piece of cake! I slithered around the empty tub on the floor and reached for the door of the camper. I pulled on it . . . and pulled on it. It was locked!

Chapter 16

"We're trapped!" I exclaimed breathlessly. I stared at Patti, horrified. Who knew what the Goodwins would do when they found us? And they were bound to find us. We couldn't live under their bed forever! Any more than Tug could live in that tub much longer.

"We can't be! Let's try a window!" Patti whispered.

I grabbed the handle of the nearest window and cranked. But the window only opened about five inches. Not even Patti was skinny enough to fit through a space that size.

"It's no good," I said. "But maybe Josh is looking this way. . . ." I was clutching at straws, but I grabbed the sweatshirt I had tied around my waist, and hung it out the window like a flag.

"Please, Josh — be looking," I begged silently. "You're our only hope!"

Of course, even if he spotted the sweatshirt, he'd have to run all the way back to Aunt Mary's to tell the others. Then they'd have to drive into Puerto Delfin for the sheriff, since the phone still wasn't working. Who knew where we'd be by then?

Patti seemed more worried about Tug than about us. "Poor baby," she said sorrowfully. "He can hardly move a muscle. He's probably been stuck in here since Josh saw that light last night. I'll bet he can't go without manatee milk much longer. And he looks so frightened."

"What about poor Patti and Stephanie?" I said, feeling pretty desperate myself. Patti didn't seem to realize how serious our situation really was.

"As soon as we get to a highway, we'll start yelling for help, Stephanie," Patti said softly. But she didn't sound all that confident.

"Patti, this crate has four-wheel drive," I pointed out. "The Goodwins could take backroads for a long time. We might never see civilization again!"

"Oh, dear," Patti said, finally beginning to get the whole awful picture. "Well, maybe Josh saw the sweatshirt."

And maybe not.

* * *

We rolled along for what seemed like a very long time — I hadn't thought to put on my watch that morning. The two of us scrunched down between the two tubs, trying to stay calm and quiet. It felt kind of comforting, having Patti's warm shoulder against mine. And Tug splashing behind us.

I was doing some hard thinking. If the Goodwins were responsible for stealing Tug, where did that leave the Marcuses? I supposed it could be possible that they were in on it — that we were heading over to connect up with them right now. But somehow I didn't think so. For one thing, Josh definitely hadn't known them. For another thing, if it had been the Goodwins with the green lights all this time, then they had been planning to steal Tug since long before the Marcuses came on the scene.

And, who had been the mysterious intruder in the woods, our first day here? There were so many unfinished ends to this mystery: Who had cut the phone wires, who had wrecked the house, why Greg Grandy was so anxious for Tara to sell. . . .

Suddenly the camper stopped so fast that Patti and I almost banged our foreheads on the tub in front of us!

"Hey! Watch it, buddy! Just where do you think you're going?" someone shouted in a very cross voice. "A guy tries to get in a jog on the beach before work, and nearly gets run over by some maniac!''

"He sounds familiar," Patti whispered.

He did to me, too! "Mr. Grandy!" I screamed, "Help! We're trapped back here!" Patti and I both hollered: "Help! Heeeeeelllp! Police!"

"Who's that?" Greg Grandy demanded.

"I don't know what you're talking about!" Mr. Goodwin snarled. Then the motor of the camper roared to life again, and we started jerking forward!

"Stop right where you are!" Mr. Grandy ordered. I couldn't believe I would ever be glad to hear his voice, but I sure was that morning. He was getting closer to us now. Then there was a loud thump.

"They've run him down!" Patti groaned.

The camper jolted to a stop again, and Mr. Goodwin yelled, "Get off the hood, you little creep!" We heard a car door being flung open, and somebody went, "Oooof!"

"They're fighting!" Patti said, squirming to her feet and trying to peer out a window.

"Watch it — I know karate!" Greg Grandy panted. "Ow!" I guess he didn't know karate very well.

I struggled to my feet and tugged at the back door with all my might, but Patti pulled me away from it. "Watch out — here comes Mrs. Goodwin!" she cried.

Mrs. Goodwin's mean face was glaring through

166

the window at us. "You troublemaking brats!" she yelled. "Now you're in for it!" There was the sound of a key in a lock, and the door was shoved open. Mrs. Goodwin started to climb into the camper with us.

"Help!" we shouted, backing up. "Somebody, please help!"

All of a sudden we heard sirens growing louder in the distance and the screech of brakes! "Hold it right there!" a voice shouted through a megaphone. "This is the police! Come out with your hands up!"

"On what charge?" growled Mrs. Goodwin, looking out the back door at him.

"Kidnapping, for starters!" Sheriff Gunn said.

"Josh saw the sweatshirt," I said weakly to Patti. My knees started to buckle as Mrs. Goodwin backed away from us. "We're saved!"

Patti and I gave each other a hug and sank down on a bunk.

Once Mrs. Goodwin was out, Sheriff Gunn came to the door and Patti and I scrambled out, too. He's a tall, broad man with a lined face and a re-assuring grin. There were three deputies waiting just outside, plus Uncle Nick and Tara, Lauren, Kate (if you can believe it, Kate was filming the whole thing!), Josh (our hero), Troy, and their parents. Greg Grandy, our second hero, was holding a handkerchief to his bleeding nose.

The Goodwins were being handcuffed, but they were scowling like they wanted to kill us.

"Those kids were trespassing — how were we supposed to know they were hiding in the camper!" Mr. Goodwin protested.

That's when Patti and I announced, "They've got an endangered baby manatee in there!"

Tara and Uncle Nick and Kate and Lauren stopped hugging us long enough to gasp, "Tug?"

"Tug," Patti and I said. "And he's been without food for hours!"

Uncle Nick and the sheriff both managed to squeeze into the camper. As soon as Sheriff Gunn took a good look at the second tub, that was the end of the Goodwins. Sheriff Gunn actually said, "Book 'em!" — just like in the movies! Then two of the deputies pushed the Goodwins into the back of a squad car!

"Thanks," I said to Josh. "You saved us."

"And you, too, Mr. Grandy," Patti added.

"No big deal," Josh said with a pleased grin.

Mr. Grandy just nodded weakly, and put the handkerchief back up to his nose.

That night at Aunt Mary's house, we had a sort of celebration dinner with Mr. Grandy and the Marcuses. As it turned out, Mr. Grandy explained that he was desperate to buy the house because his grandfather, who had been one of the first architects in Puerto Delfin, had designed it. That was one mystery cleared up.

"That's a great story, Greg, but after this thrilling vacation, I know I couldn't part with the house," Tara said, laughing.

Thrilling? And guess what? The Marcuses *weren't* endangered-animal thieves. They're sea mammal experts at the San Diego Zoo and they were at Wonderworld to try to acquire a manatee!

I felt pretty silly when I thought about how much I had suspected them. And how much time I had wasted being suspicious of Josh. Especially since he'd saved our lives.

We also learned that the intruder we saw that first day had been Carl Withers! He'd been using our beach to sunbathe on. So Tara had been right.

After dinner, Sheriff Gunn stopped by to give us the scoop on the Goodwins.

"They're just a couple of shady characters, traveling around the country, grabbing what they can to sell," the sheriff said. "The Goodwins spotted this empty house, set way off by itself, and decided to clean it out."

"They're the ones who cut the phone wires and stole the furniture?" asked Tara.

"That's right — they unloaded it at the auction near Jacksonville. They used false names, of course, but the auctioneer recognized their pictures," Sheriff Gunn replied. "Once he'd identified them — and we found the rubber boots that matched your notched footprint in the camper — the Goodwins spilled the beans. They had even moved into this house for a while."

"That's when the ghost rumors started?" I interrupted.

"Yep. People saw their flashlights. When the Goodwins heard about the rumors, they added to them — to ensure their privacy while they burglarized more places up and down the coast," Sheriff Gunn said.

"And then they spotted our manatees," said Uncle Nick.

Sheriff Gunn nodded. "They figured they'd make lots more money out of manatees than old furniture. There are a few unscrupulous private collectors around who'll pay a bundle for exotic animals."

"Even if they're endangered?" Kate said indignantly.

"Especially if they're endangered," the sheriff replied. "Then they just keep them for their own enjoyment. Kind of like people who buy stolen paintings so famous that they can never show them to anyone. Unfortunately. Anyway, that narrow creek out there was the perfect place for the Goodwins to net a manatee or two. They hadn't given a thought to the fact that the manatees might die in the process."

And that's pretty much the end of the story. It had also been the Goodwins who had wrecked the house when we were at Wonderworld. They had wanted to scare us off because they knew they had to capture Tug soon.

Speaking of Tug, as soon as the Goodwins had been loaded into the squad car that morning, Sheriff Gunn had driven the camper right into the jungle to the creek. He, Uncle Nick, Mr. Marcus, and the boys lifted Tug out of the tub, rolled him up in one of the Goodwins' blankets, and carried him back to his mom. While we watched, the two manatees rubbed noses and patted each other with their flippers. Then they frolicked off, farther up the creek, with a splash and a couple of flips.

Now, I have to get back to my Florida vacation — Josh is waiting for us to get ready to go to the reef! I have to cram a lot of fun into our few remaining days. Oh — a couple of other things. Uncle Nick says we'll have to come up with another name for our baby manatee. . . . He's pretty sure Tug is a girl! And a news team is coming down here to film our story for national TV! Best of all, the bus company *promises* that my suitcase will be here tomorrow! Suitcase? What suitcase?

Sleepover Friends, forever!

#38 Patti's City Adventure

"Are you sure they're not still here somewhere?" I asked Stephanie. We had looked all over the street for Patti and Lauren, but it was pretty obvious they were gone.

"Kate, we've looked everywhere but under the manholes," Stephanie said with a sigh. "They're on that bus!"

I snapped my fingers. "I know what we should do! Let's take a cab after the bus."

"That won't work," Stephanie replied.

"Sure it will! People do it in the movies all the time. We just get in a cab and say, 'Follow that bus!'"

"It might have worked if we'd done it five minutes ago," said Stephanie. "But that bus is long gone!"